MURDER

— ON THE —

MOOR

A Rex Graves Mystery

MURDER
— ON THE —
MOOR

C. S. Challinor

MIDNIGHT INK
WOODBURY, MINNESOTA

FIRST EDITION
First Printing, 2011

Book design by Donna Burch
Cover design by Kevin R. Brown
Cover photo illustration © Kevin R.Brown; Cottage © iStockphoto.com/Lee Rogers;
    Scottish Highlands © iStockphoto.com/Matthew Dixon
Editing by Connie Hill

Midnight Ink, an imprint of Llewellyn Worldwide Ltd.

Library of Congress Cataloging-in-Publication Data

Challinor, C. S. (Caroline S.)
  Murder on the moor / C.S. Challinor. — 1st ed.
      p.   cm. — (A Rex Graves mystery ; no. 4)
  ISBN 978-0-7387-1981-8
  1. Graves, Rex (Fictitious character)—Fiction. 2. Murder—Investigation—
Fiction. 3. Scotland—Fiction. I. Title.
  PS3603.H3366M89   2011
  813'.6—dc22   2010043964

Midnight Ink
A Division of Llewellyn Worldwide Ltd.
2143 Wooddale Drive
Woodbury, MN 55125-2989
www.midnightinkbooks.com

Printed in the United States of America

CAST OF MAIN CHARACTERS

Rex Graves—Scottish barrister and amateur sleuth, new and proud owner of Gleneagle Lodge

Chief Inspector Dalgerry—of Central Scotland Police, who heads up the Moor Murders investigation

Detective Inspector Strickler—Dalgerry's skeptical subordinate

Detective Sergeant Dawes—Strickler's younger partner

HOUSE GUESTS

Helen d'Arcy—Rex Graves' current love interest

Cuthbert Farquharson—trigger-happy laird

Estelle Farquharson—Cuthbert's snobby, gossipy wife

Alistair Frazer—Rex Graves' dashing and enigmatic colleague

Hamish Allerdice—local hotelier with wandering hands

Shona Allerdice—Hamish's furtive wife

Donnie Allerdice—son with learning disabilities

Flora Allerdice—Donnie's devoted and tragic sister

Rob Roy Beardsley—zealous freelance journalist

Moira Wilcox—Rex Graves' previous love interest

ONE

"It's a pig in a poke," the first McCallum decreed, shaking his head dubiously at the cast-iron radiator in the guest bedroom of Rex's converted hunting lodge.

"Aye," agreed McCallum's equally stout younger brother. "Ye should hae switched to contemporary models," he told Rex, "like we said when ye first purchased this place. These old radiators retain more heat, but if this'un continues to leak, you'll end up wi' a rotten floorboard. The radiator is so corroded it could come off the wall and fall onto somebody's heed."

"I like these radiators," Rex protested. "They have character."

"Ye canna let emotion get in the way of good sense," the first McCallum chided, looking at Rex as though he were a clueless twit and not a preeminent Scottish barrister. "Now, it can be fixed—if yer heart is set on it, but it will cost ye."

"Aye," seconded the brother. "Parts are dear. Not many of these radiators left around the country."

"Why can't you just solder the damn thing?"

With exaggerated patience, the elder McCallum launched into an ABC of plumbing basics.

"How long to fix it?" Rex finally asked. "I have guests arriving this afternoon."

"Och, it canna be done afore then," the elder McCallum exclaimed. "Ye'll have to keep the pan there to collect the water until we can get back sometime next week."

This was not reassuring, especially the "sometime next week" part. The local labor force adhered to the typical Highland attitude toward work: It would get done when desire for food or whisky absolutely drove them to the necessity of it, and not before.

"Now, take heed," the younger brother said. "The leak will likely get worse, so I suggest ye get a bigger pan."

"We'll take fifty pounds now for the consultation," the other said. "Ta verra much, squire," he added as he pocketed the money in greedy anticipation of an afternoon at the pub.

Rex was now anxious to get the two men out of the lodge before Helen returned from the village shop and saw the mud they had tracked up the stairs on their work boots. She was as industrious and house-proud as a badger and had spent the past two days sprucing up the place in preparation for the housewarming party.

He felt less enthusiastic about the proceedings. The whole point of the lodge, after all, had been for them to spend time together by themselves. A stroke of luck had brought him to this property near Inverness, a couple of hours' drive north of Edinburgh, where he lived.

It might seem odd and slightly suspect to some people that a mature man would live at home with an aging, if still sprightly parent, but the arrangement had made sense when Rex lost his wife to cancer. He had not wanted his son, then fifteen, coming home from school to an empty house, and so he had moved back in with his mother. Now that Campbell was away at college in Florida, Rex felt an increasing desire to spread his wings.

After mopping up the mess on the stairs, he wandered down the path to wait for Helen at the gate. The stone lodge stood sideways to the loch, which at first sight seemed odd, but in fact was quite logical. Logic always counted more for Rex than aesthetics and may have been the reason the Victorian hunting lodge had not been snapped up sooner.

The front door—at the side of the house—faced north toward the village of Gleneagle. The conservatory built onto the south side hoarded any sun the thrifty Highland summer deigned to bestow within its glass walls and looked upon a garden carpeted with bluebells and hedged by late-flowering rhododendrons and azaleas.

The best view, though, was reserved for the living room, whose large windows opened onto the loch. This is where the logic of the architect back in 1845 came into play, for Loch Lown comprised only a narrow body of water, not much wider than the breadth of the house, and by positioning the lodge in this perpendicular manner, the most important rooms embraced a long perspective of the lake.

Gleneagle Lodge was the only residence on the mile-long loch, which had once belonged to the laird of Gleneagle Castle, now a tattered ruin at the top of the hill in the direction of the village. Parcels of the estate had been successively sold off to honor the debts of the dissolute Fraser family, distant relations of the famous clan of that name, until the grounds had shrunk to the confines of the four-bedroom lodge, loch, and several hundred acres of hill and glen, currently in the proud possession of Rex Graves, Queen's Counsel.

The loch, though not large, was deep, and believed to connect by means of underwater tunnels via Loch Lochy, a neighboring lake, to Loch Ness. Fortunately for Rex, Loch Lown was off the beaten path and sunk amid steep pinewood hills surmountable only by one axle-breaking road or by the most energetic of hikers. Rex hoped his ubiquitous "Private Property—Keep Off" and "Deer Stalking Strictly Prohibited" signs would further deter the public from venturing onto his land.

He spotted a figure cresting the hill and, minutes later, the form of Helen appeared carrying a basket. He started out on the single-track road and began climbing. The foothills bloomed with purple heather. The sunlight filtering between the pine trees warmed his shoulders. It would have been perfect weather were the air not rife with biting midges, the curse of Highland summers. Swatting them from his face, he smiled up at Helen as she plunged down the hill, her tweed skirt flopping above her knees, wisps of blond hair falling in her laughing blue eyes.

"I saw the McCallum van," she said as they met up on the road. "Did they fix the radiator?"

He would have gladly joined her on her walk to the village but for the appointment with the builders, which had been set for "sometime in the day."

"No, but they still managed to get a fifty out of me."

"Oh, Rex, you should have let me deal with them."

Helen was a practical woman and probably would not have put up with any nonsense from the McCallum brothers, but Rex felt it was a man's place to deal with loutish contractors.

"I suppose they drew sharp intakes of breath and heaved deep sighs of woe when they inspected the radiator," she added.

"Aye, pretty much."

"And they said it would cost an arm and a leg to fix anything so antiquated."

"They did, only they didn't express themselves in such eloquent terms." He took Helen's basket and they walked toward the lodge gate.

"I know how you feel about supporting the local economy, Rex, but I think they are taking advantage."

"Aye, but they're right clannish around here. If I hired a townie, I'd be shunned by the whole village. They'd put a hex on those eggs you bought."

Helen laughed outright. "You're just a big-hearted softie. I cannot imagine you sending people off to prison."

"It's my job."

"When are they coming back to fix it?"

"Next week," Rex said with a conviction he did not feel.

"Ah, well, at least no one will be using that room. It's only Alistair and the Farquharsons staying over, isn't it?"

Rex groaned at the thought. The Farquharsons were horrible snobs, but they had contributed ostentatiously to his mother's pet missionary charity and she had insisted he put them up for a few days. Alistair was a colleague from the High Court of Justiciary, the supreme criminal court of Scotland, and had given him the tip about Gleneagle Lodge, having heard of the sale from a solicitor friend.

"Who else did you say was coming?" Helen asked.

"The Allerdice couple who own a hotel on Loch Lochy on the other side of Deer Glen. They're bringing their son and daughter. Donnie has a learning disability. The lass is a bit of a wallflower. The parents are anxious to marry her off."

Helen rolled her eyes. "How feudal."

"They asked if they could bring a guest from the hotel. He's writing an article on Lizzie, Loch Lochy's answer to Nessie of Loch Ness fame. I gather the plesiosaurs are cousins, or some such nonsense."

"Oh, I heard all about that at the village shop. Old Cameron spotted Lizzie this morning when he was fishing for pike. He said the creature fits the description of the Loch Ness monster, only it's smaller."

"It'll grow by the end of the night," Rex predicted. "That story will be worth a few drams at the pub."

"Isn't it exciting? A prehistoric monster living in the neighbouring loch!"

"Och, c'mon, now—it's a big hoax!"

They reached the side of the lodge, with its red gingerbread gable culminating in a generous chimney. The newly varnished oak door formed the only aperture in the gray stone wall. Flanked by two huge pots of geraniums, it displayed a brass knocker and a plaque engraved with "R. Graves" above the letter box, leaving no doubt as to the main entry to the house. Previously, visitors had wandered about in some confusion, peering into downstairs windows, much to Rex's annoyance.

"Well, I best get on with my cake," Helen said. "What time will they be arriving?"

"Around six." Rex wondered if he should change out of his corduroys, and decided he couldn't be bothered. "Can I do anything to help?"

"It's all taken care of, except for the smoked salmon canopies. But you can keep me company in the kitchen if you want."

"I'd rather keep you company somewhere else," Rex growled. "I do wish these people weren't coming."

"Oh, come on, Rex. It'll be *fun*."

At that moment, he heard the rumble of an engine on the other side of the hill and seconds later saw a Land Rover hurtling down the incline. An arm shot out of the passenger window waving a bright scarf, followed by a middle-aged aristocratic face framed by beige, shoulder-length hair.

"Well, he-llo!" Mrs. Farquharson bleated. "We found you!"

Worst luck, Rex thought.

The next moment he was introducing Estelle and Cuthbert Farquharson to Helen.

"*Ceud mile failte*," Helen welcomed them. "I've been practicing my Scottish Gaelic."

Cuthbert babbled some incomprehensible Gaelic politeness in reply before turning to Rex. "I say, I thought we'd get in a bit of deer stalking." He clapped Rex on the back. "Plenty of time before dinner, what?"

Cuthbert Farquharson sported a Sherlock Holmes deerstalker and matching camouflage trousers bagging over sage green rubber boots. Estelle also wore wellies, along with a sloppy sweater and frumpy tweed skirt, the attire of landed gentry. Though Scottish, they had both been educated in England, Estelle at some highfaluting London school and Cuthbert at Eton, which accounted for their horsy accents.

"How bloody marvelous this place is," Estelle remarked prior to inhaling deeply of the pure, pine-scented air. "So wild and unspoilt." She cast a determined look at the lodge, apparently undaunted by the idea of "slumming it" and prepared for any eventuality. "Doesn't look like anything's changed much over the centuries. It's so *authentic!*"

"We do have indoor plumbing," Rex countered mildly. "In fact, all modern conveniences." Then, remembering the leaking radiator, he added, "Of sorts."

"Your room is all ready for you," Helen told the guests. "I was just about to bake a cake."

"A cake! How fabulous!" Estelle enthused.

"With real eggs, fresh from the local farm," Rex added with a straight face.

"Divine. Do let me help."

"Good idea." Cuthbert prodded his wife in Helen's direction. "The ghillie should be here in a minute with the pony," he told Rex.

"What ghillie?"

"The boy from the Loch Lochy Hotel. His parents and sister will be along later with that reporter chap."

"We won't be needing a ghillie or a pony," Rex said firmly. "We won't be shooting any deer."

Ponies were still the transportation of choice for retrieving dead deer over hilly terrain.

"But I brought my new rifle. Thought I'd try it out."

"The only thing we shoot here are photographs," Rex explained.

A deer head replete with a pair of seven-pointed antlers had hung forlornly over the living room fireplace when he purchased the lodge. The first thing he had done was to give it a decent burial and replace it with a copy of *Monarch of the Glen*, the famous oil painting of a majestic stag by nineteenth-century artist Sir Edwin Landseer.

"Did you bring a camera?" he asked his guest.

"Estelle has a Nikon somewhere." Cuthbert's bottom lip, wet and red as a woman's, trembled peevishly. "Not quite the same thing, is it?"

"I don't believe in murdering God's creatures for sport."

"You can't view them as defenseless bambies, you know. They wreak havoc with the forests. Without wolves to cull the population, it's the best way to keep the numbers under control."

Rex shook his head resolutely. "Not on my land. I like to think of Gleaneagle Lodge as a nature sanctuary."

At that moment, a golden eagle swooped overhead and soared over the barren hill summits.

"Well, it's your land, I suppose, and you're free to do with it as you please," Cuthbert conceded. "Here's the boy now."

An uneven clopping of hooves rang out as Donnie Allerdice, an agile lad of about seventeen in a plaid shirt and jeans, led a sturdy Shetland pony down the loose stone road.

"This here is Honey," he told the men when he drew level with them. "On account of the colour of her coat, not her temperament." He said this in a slow and deliberate way. The horse chewed irritably on its bit and twitched its long tail. "The midges are bothering her something fierce."

"You can put her in the meadow over there for the time being," Rex told the boy, who was slightly cross-eyed. "We won't be needing her."

"Mr. Graves is opposed to hunting," Cuthbert explained testily.

"That's a shame," the boy said. "I saw a large hummel and his hinds down in the glen." Rex noticed he carried a sheath knife in his belt.

"A hummel, eh?" Cuthbert questioned. "Those are pretty rare. They don't grow antlers," he told Rex. "I wouldn't mind taking a look. Could you show me?" he asked the boy.

Rex reached out for the rifle. "Before you go, could you leave this? I'll put it in the house."

Cuthbert reluctantly handed it over. A military-looking telescopic lens was mounted on the gun. Rex reflected that a deer would never stand a chance against such a state-of-the-art example of ruthless weaponry.

He had better put it somewhere safe.

TWO

Rex felt glad to be rid of Cuthbert for a while and hoped the hummel would lead him on a wild goose chase. He deposited the rifle upstairs in a cupboard in the bedroom with the leaky radiator and went to see how Helen was getting on in the kitchen. He was very proud of his kitchen, which retained its flagstone floor and Victorian tile-work, but where he had updated the cabinetry and installed a vintage Aga stove re-enameled in red.

Helen and Estelle were whisking up a storm at the granite island countertop. A bottle of sherry stood open before them.

"Are you making sherry trifle?" he asked.

"The sherry is for us," Helen explained. "The cooks' prerogative. Would you like a glass?"

"I'll hold off for now, thanks. Having fun?"

"Oh, Helen and I are getting on like a house on fire," Estelle enthused. "She was just telling me how you two met in Sussex two Christmases ago when you were solving your first private case. How absolutely thrilling!" Mrs. Farquharson wiped her hands on a flowery apron and chugged down some sherry. "You solved the case of the missing actress in the Caribbean too, didn't you?" The question was more of a statement, and so he refrained from confirming.

"There was a piece about it on BBC Scotland," Helen told her. "Rex did an interview."

Rex coughed modestly.

"Any other private cases in the works?" Estelle asked.

"I hope not," he said. "I have my plate full as it is what with this place and my day job."

"You've done wonders with Gleaneagle Lodge. Helen showed me the before-and-after pictures. I hope you'll have many happy times here together. Cheers." Estelle raised her glass in a toast.

"Thank you. Is that someone at the door?" Certain that he had heard the doorbell, Rex stepped into the hall.

"Alistair!" he exclaimed upon opening the front door. He gladly accepted his colleague's gift of a bottle of Glenlivet. "Glad you could make it. Come on through to the library. The women are busy in the kitchen."

"You've done a lot to this place," Alistair remarked, looking about him. "I like what you did to the front, or is it the back? I suppose the front is the loch view, right?"

Alistair Frazer, a man blessed with distinguished good looks and sartorial flair, sank into one of the wing armchairs by an open fireplace, where the unlit logs were piled for effect. His hair, beginning to recede at the temples, trailed in loose curls to the nape of his neck, giving him a Byronic look. His wan cheeks added to his romantic and melancholy air.

"It was a lot of work," Rex acknowledged, taking a seat opposite him and contemplating with satisfaction the recently stained wood-paneled walls. "How was your trip up?"

"Just fine. I took my time. I drove past Rannoch Moor." Alistair's face grew somber above his peach-hued cravat. "It's right desolate. Just miles and miles of windswept peat and bog."

"Now, don't go punishing yourself," Rex counseled. "You did your best."

His barrister colleague had recently prosecuted a child molestation and murder case at the High Court of Justiciary in Edinburgh, and had lost. The victim's body had been found on Rannoch Moor.

"It was airtight," Alistair groaned. "Collins' blood was found on the wee girl's body."

"The defense argued that he found her after the fact and scratched himself on the brambles while trying to lift her out of the bog." Rex had not been in court for the trial but had followed the proceedings with interest. The Kirsty MacClure case had been all over the media. Two previous child murders on the moor in the past two years had not turned up any suspects.

"It had to have been him," Alistair persisted. "There was no one else around for miles. Every square kilometer was searched from Glen Moor Village to Abercroft."

"I know." Rex shoved a hand through his hair in frustration. "That Kilfarley is a good defense lawyer. Collins was lucky to get him."

"It's a shame we couldn't get in his previous arrest for child molestation. Kirsty's murder had his modus operandi all over it."

"Possibly, but he had an alibi for the time of death. The jury rightly decided they couldn't risk sending an innocent man to prison."

"Innocent, my eye. Now he's free and there's a huge outcry that the culprit hasn't been caught. Parents are not letting their bairns out to play. Just wait until another child is abducted, strangled by their own underwear. It's only a matter of time." Alistair suddenly fell silent as Helen entered the room.

"Tea, anyone? Nice to see you again, Alistair."

"Thanks, lass." He gave Helen a friendly wink.

"Aye, don't mind if I do," Rex said.

"You both look like somebody died." When neither of the men said anything, she added, "Well, tea it is, then," and left the room.

"Nice woman, your Helen," Alistair murmured. "Cheerful and wholesome."

"She is that."

"Do you discuss your trial cases with her?"

"Not usually. We don't get to see each other that much, what with her living in Derby, so I prefer to keep off the subject of work, especially when it involves something as upsetting as the Kirsty MacClure murder."

"If Collins ever crosses my path, I'll take justice into my own hands, just mark my words."

"That's no way for an advocate to talk, Alistair," Rex said in a conciliatory manner. "You did your utmost."

Rex really couldn't fault him for his attitude though. Of the serious crimes that came before the High Court, violence against children was the most heinous and hardest to forget. He hoped the housewarming party would help take Alistair's mind off the case.

"Did I tell you the Allerdices are coming?" he asked. "You've met them, I think."

"Aye, a couple of times when I was staying at the hotel with Bill." Bill Menzies was the solicitor who had arranged the sale of Gleneagle Lodge. "I saw the Allerdice boy walking over the ridge when I was driving over. He was with a man in full deer-stalking regalia."

"Cuthbert Farquharson."

"The laird of Aberleven in Fife?" Alistair asked in disgust. "That Tory philanthropist who lent his party two million pounds? What's he doing here?"

Rex leaned forward. "I'm afraid he's one of our house guests. I bought this place so I could get away from snobs like that, but he and his wife, Estelle, gave generously to my mother's charity."

"Supplying bibles to illiterate tribes in the Amazonian jungle, when we're trying to conserve their trees?" Alistair joked.

"Aye, well Mother supports missionary work and she insisted I invite the Farquharsons here since they were in Inverness."

Helen came back into the library with a tray of crockery and a plate of perfectly cut cucumber sandwiches. "The Allerdices rang to say they were running a bit late. Their guest, Mr. Beardsley, got delayed on a hike, but they're on their way, with their daughter."

"Flora's a sweet thing," Alistair said as Helen knelt at an end table to pour the tea. "Devoted to her younger brother, Donnie. He's a bit slow."

"You mean mentally disabled?" asked Helen, who had no patience for euphemisms. Her forthrightness was one of the many things Rex appreciated about her.

"Aye, but only mildly."

"I noticed something amiss with the lad," Rex acknowledged. "It's hard to tell if he's actually looking at you. And he punctuates every word with a pause."

"Forest Gump," Helen said. It was one of her favorite movies.

"Exactly. He seems like a nice lad."

Helen handed out cups and poured one for herself. "Estelle's upstairs freshening up."

"How did it go in the kitchen?" Rex asked.

"Oh, fine. She's quite tipsy though. I hope she makes it through the rest of the evening. What's Mrs. Allerdice like?"

The two men looked at each other, seeking inspiration.

"Mousy," Alistair ventured. "You'd better watch out for her husband."

"Oh? Why?"

"Hamish can't keep his hands off attractive women."

Helen laughed. "Rex will protect my honour."

At that moment, the slamming of car doors reached Rex's ears. The last of the guests had arrived. He rose from his comfortable armchair with a resigned sigh. "Looks like rain," he forecast, pausing before the library window. The slate-gray loch across the grass mirrored a glowering sky.

"The weatherman on the car radio announced heavy rain, perhaps even hail," Alistair informed him.

"That's a shame," Helen stood up and rearranged her skirt. "We were hoping to entertain our guests in the garden."

"No hope of that," Rex said, making for the door. "We just got our first drops."

He desperately hoped there would not be a rainstorm. He did not want his newest guests outstaying their welcome.

THREE

Rex crossed the hall and went outside to greet the newcomers. Shona Allerdice, under the shelter of an umbrella held by her husband, scurried toward the stone porch with a huge casserole in her arms.

"Just in time," she cried as the deluge began.

Rex ushered them inside and, borrowing the umbrella, ran over to the van to get Flora. The young woman scrambled out the back door carrying two bottles of red wine, her patent leather shoes totally inappropriate for the weather, Rex noted. A bearded and bespectacled man in his thirties exited on the other side with a knapsack.

"Don't worry about me," he said, indicating the umbrella in Rex's hand. "I'm used to being out in all weather. I'm Rob Roy, by the way. Staying at the hotel."

The three of them made a dash for the front door.

"We best all take off our shoes," Mrs. Allerdice suggested, removing her medium-heeled pumps.

She was, as Alistair had described her, a mousy woman, with a pinched face. Flora would resemble her mother in twenty years, Rex mused, but for now she had youth on her side. She wore her dull brown hair in a headband. Both women were narrow in the shoulder and wide at the hip, and dowdily dressed.

Rex appreciated Shona's consideration regarding the footwear. He had already had to clean up after the two workmen, and Beardsley's walking shoes were covered in mud.

"Hope you like Burgundy," Hamish Allerdice said in a gruff Scottish accent, taking the wine bottles off his daughter. "It'll go superbly with the venison stew we brought. It's our chef's special."

"Most kind," Rex murmured. He detested venison. It was too gamey for his taste, and he could never eat it without thinking of the noble beast twitching its nose in the air, alert to danger but blind to its source.

"Your son went off with one of my guests to stalk a hummel," he told Allerdice. "I hope they find shelter from the rain."

"Donnie will know what to do," Flora reassured him. "He's right at home in the ootdoors. Is the pony with them?"

"No, she's in the meadow. I should put her in the stable now that it's raining down hard."

"I'll do it," Beardsley offered. "I'm already wet, and Honey knows me."

Rex walked back out with him onto the covered stone porch. The stable could accommodate four horses. He had cleaned it out and whitewashed it, and was using it for storage. The gardener had stacked hay in one of the stalls when he cut the grass.

"You'll find a bucket in there," Rex told Beardsley. "A hose is attached to the wall if you need to give her water." He had no clue about horses.

"Terrific. There's some oats in the van I can feed her."

"Hurry back." Rex patted the man on the shoulder. "There's plenty of drink and food for us too."

Helen had set up a buffet in the living room overlooking the loch, the view transformed into a blur of rain. Rex decided to light the fire to provide a more hospitable atmosphere on this drab evening.

"Here, let me do that, lass," he said to Helen who was opening bottles at the drinks cabinet. "You've done more than enough already."

"All right. I'll go circulate."

He poured malt whisky for Alistair and Mr. Allerdice. "It's raining on my parade," he commented with a rueful glance out the window.

"Not to worry," Hamish Allerdice replied. "We're spoilt enough with views over our own loch, don't you think, Alistair? You've visited Loch Lochy."

"Aye, the view from the hotel dining room is spectacular."

"One of our guests saw the sea monster a couple of weeks ago," Hamish boasted. "Our waiter saw it as well. Thought at first it was an upturned boat, but then he spotted three humps and a tail. We sent a photo to the *Inverness News-Press*, and Rob Roy came to check it out."

"It was probably a couple of seals frolicking in the water," Rex opined.

"It had the same sleek head, but it was twelve foot long."

Rex took a closer look at Hamish Allerdice. Nondescript like his wife and prey to the signs of male middle age: thinning hair, thickening midsection, pouchy eyes, and jowly cheeks. Rex commended himself that his own sandstone red hair had stayed intact. Moreover, his bulky frame carried his surplus weight better than Hamish's shorter stature. *Vanity, thy name is Man!* he chided himself.

"There was another sighting this morning," Helen said, joining the men, a glass of sherry in her hand. "They were talking about it at the village shop."

"Aye, that's right." Hamish's eyes lingered on her bust, accentuated by the black halter-neck dress she had changed into upstairs. "Rob Roy wants to interview the old fisherman. Cameron is a local attraction in his own right."

The journalist entered the room with Cuthbert Farquharson and the adolescent boy, Donnie. Flora jumped to her brother's side and started fussing over him, pulling the scarf from his neck and using it to mop his face and dark hair. Divested of his deerstalker, Farquharson's fading blond curls hung limply over his forehead.

"Come and dry yourselves by the fire," Rex invited.

He crossed to the stereo system and put on a CD of Scottish ballads, which seemed appropriate for the mournful weather. The logs in the fireplace caught flame from the pine kindling and began to blaze cheerfully. Tongues, loosened by alcohol, spoke louder, everyone talking at once about the Loch Lochy phenomenon, which Shona Allerdice said would undoubtedly drum up business for the hotel.

"We're having a slow season," her husband explained.

"The creature is naught but a gimmick," Rex remarked in response to the Allerdices' comments, his Scots coming out stronger as always in times of emotion. "It's bad enough hearing all the nonsense aboot Nessie, but now *Lizzie?* Is every loch going to produce its own sea monster?"

Helen laughed. "Oh, Rex, you should be proud of your monsters."

"I'm proud of Bonnie Prince Charlie, John Knox, Robbie Burns, and all the rest o' them, and of our turbulent and bloody heritage—not of two-headed freaks of nature lurking in every puddle."

"It's not two-headed," Shona Allerdice corrected him. "It's a wonderful creature that resembles a serpent, only with flippers and three humps on its back. There's loads of data proving the existence of a Loch Ness monster. It even has a scientific Latin name, but I forget what it is."

"*Nessiteras rhombopteryx,*" Rex supplied.

"You see, you're more informed about it than you like to admit," Helen cried out with glee. She turned to Shona. "I'd love to catch a glimpse of it to show the boys and girls at my school." She glanced at her slim gold watch. "Oops, I should go and check on the quiche."

"Rob Roy is writing an article on our Lizzie," Shona told Rex proudly. He's staying at our hotel while he finishes his research. He may even end up writing a book about it. That would definitely put the Loch Lochy Hotel on the map."

Rex mentally rolled his eyes. *Try serving better food and refurbishing the place with less hokey décor,* he thought. He had stayed at the Loch Lochy Hotel while work was going on at the lodge, since it was conveniently close. It was not somewhere he would stay by choice.

Rob Roy Beardsley nodded in agreement with Shona. "This may be only the tip of the iceberg. There have been sightings of a third monster in this verra loch."

"My loch?" Rex said, aghast at the thought.

"Aye, Loch Lown. *Lown* means 'serene' in Scottish dialect. Did you ken that?"

"It won't remain serene for long once news of a monster breaks out," Rex remonstrated. "Please don't write anything aboot it in your article."

Beardsley sighed with regret. "It's my journalistic obligation to inform the public."

"I suppose this third monster already has a name?" Rex inquired.

"Bessie."

"Bessie?"

"She may be a first cousin of Nessie."

"This is ridiculous."

"It's fascinating, really. Loch Ness lies along the same fault line as Lochs Lochy and Lown, and connects with them under water. The sedimentary rock which cradles the lochs is among the oldest in the world. During the last Ice Age, the deep freshwater lochs never froze, providing a safe haven for a certain species of dinosaur. And so Nessie, Bessie, and Lizzie live to tell the tale."

"My loch is technically a *lochan*—a wee loch," Rex insisted, turning to face Beardsley full on. "It's too shallow to be connected to anything. It has no outlet anywhere."

"Have you scuba dived to see what may be hidden below?"

22

"It's too murky."

"My point exactly." The journalist smiled owlishly beneath his spectacles. "You see! You never know…"

What rubbish, Rex thought, anxious to end the conversation. He saw his homeland as a serious place, full of dour Scots and revered customs. The idea of cartoonish reptiles residing in the Highland lochs made a mockery of everything that was essentially Scotland. Bad enough that the legend of Loch Ness generated a steady influx of tourists who cared less about the tragic Battle of Culloden fought not far from the shores of Loch Ness and snapped up Jurassic-style souvenirs from Drumnadrochit Village with greater ferocity than any prehistoric eel… The idea that they might start trickling across to his side of the Great Glen was frankly disturbing.

"I hope you're joking," he grumbled. "Do you write for the tabloids?"

"I'm a freelance writer for papers like the *Inverness News-Press*." Beardsley's tinny voice rose higher in pitch. "I am methodical in my research and take my profession very seriously."

"Aye, so what else have you written aboot?"

Beardsley listed a couple of nature and hiking periodicals, which Rex had never heard of.

"Monks at Fort Augustus Abbey gathered evidence of a sea dragon on Loch Lochy in 1933," Shona said in defense of her monster.

"Everyone, come and help yourselves while the food's still hot," Helen interrupted, holding an asparagus quiche between two oven gloves. She placed it on a mat on the buffet table and cast a loving eye over the tasty array of dishes displayed on the beige linen tablecloth edged in Irish lace, a housewarming gift from Rex's mother.

"What took so long?" Rex asked, taking Helen aside for a kiss.

"Cuthbert was teaching me some Gaelic in the kitchen."

"What else was he doing?" Rex asked suspiciously.

"Well, he did pinch my bottom, but I smacked his hand firmly and called him a naughty boy. Unfortunately, he seemed to like that."

"The perv. He's as bad as Hamish Allerdice."

"Anyway, before I forget what it is I'm supposed to ask you..." Helen drew herself up straight and announced, "*Cò an caora sin còmhla riut a chunnaic mi an-raoir?*"

"And what do you suppose that means?" Rex inquired.

"It means, 'How are you enjoying the party?'"

"It does not. It means, 'Who was that sheep I saw you with last night?'"

"I didn't know you spoke Gaelic!"

"I don't. I'm a Lowlander, but it's a common joke. Verra common," Rex added.

Helen burst out laughing. "I've been had! Oh, that's so funny. 'Who's that sheep I saw you with last night?' Ha, ha!"

"Go back to Cuthbert and say, from me, '*Cha b'e sin caora, 'se sin do chèile a bha innte.*' At least, I think that's right."

"What does that mean?"

"'That was no sheep, that was your wife.'"

Helen let out a whoop of laughter. Immediately her hand went to her mouth as she tried to control herself. "Oh, I'm sorry, but—Estelle does look like a sheep!"

Estelle Farquharson, who had changed into a magenta frock, came up to them with her long, ovine face and asked horsily, "What on earth is so amusing?"

"I—um—er—your husband just told me a joke," Helen replied, wiping tears from her eyes.

"Really? He's not usually so funny. Do tell."

"I—I can't remember!"

"What? You said he had just told you it."

"I know, but it was in Gaelic." Helen looked helplessly at Rex.

"It's not for delicate wee ears like yours," Rex told Estelle, propelling her toward the drinks cabinet. "What's your poison?"

"Oh, really! I may be an aristocrat," Estelle said coyly, "but I grew up with three brothers, you know."

Rex had to refrain from looking at her. She really did resemble a sheep with her woolly hair.

He gazed around the room to make sure everyone had what they needed. The Allerdices and Rob Roy Beardsley stood to one corner, no doubt devising ways to capitalize on Liz of Loch Lochy. Rex wondered if Beardsley was getting free room and board out of the deal.

The Allerdice children, Flora and Donnie, perched close together on a window seat with plates of food on their laps. Rex poured himself a small tumbler of the Glenlivet that Alistair had brought and made his way back to Helen.

"Flora is a martyr to her brother," she said, glancing in the direction of the siblings.

"I wonder if having a slow-witted brother under her wing has cramped her style at all."

"Possibly, but she's not very extrovert to begin with."

Rex held the rim of his glass to his lips, nosing the clean, oaky fragrance of the twelve-year-old single malt in anticipation of the first sip. "She could be bonny enough, but there is something lackluster aboot her. Falling in love would bring a glow to her cheeks."

"And how would you know?" Helen asked.

"Well, look at you. You are positively radiant!"

"I see," she said with an amused smile. "And I suppose you are taking all the credit? Perhaps it has something to do with the bracing walk to the village this afternoon."

"Och, noo. Fresh air just lends a ruddy sort of glow. Yours definitely comes from within." He stuck his nose back in his tumbler. Hmm. Definitely oaky, with perhaps just a hint of the heathery outdoors?

"Well, you look positively pink yourself," Helen quipped. "Of course, that might have something to do with the booze!"

Rex chuckled. He was beginning to enjoy himself, in spite of his motley crew of guests. The isolating rain lent a sense of camaraderie, and the Speyside whisky was damn good. He must remember to thank Alistair again.

"Well, doesn't look like I'll get an admission of love from you tonight," Helen groused in jest. "Might as well get back to the kitchen and see to dessert."

Rex grabbed her as she walked away and, whisking her around, planted a big kiss on her lips. "Will that do ye?" he asked.

"For now," she replied, smiling as she flounced off toward the door.

"Aye, verra nice," Hamish growled at his side, appearing out of nowhere, his gaze level with Helen's shapely behind.

Rex forced himself to restrain from decking him. Hamish Aller-dice was decidedly the most uncouth of men. And his wife in the same room, not to mention his daughter!

"Funny," his colleague Alistair said behind him. "I thought I heard someone at the door. Are you expecting more guests?"

"No, I'm not." Rex could not think whom it might be at this hour. There was no one around for miles and it was pouring with rain.

FOUR

Moira Wilcox stood under the porch with the rain hissing behind her as taillights disappeared over the hill. Dazed by a sensation of déjà-vu, Rex simply stared at her. Her dark, wavy hair glistened with moisture. Droplets of rain beaded the shoulders of her camel-hair coat. She deposited a small suitcase by the door. He took in these details one by one, his thought processes lagging behind his powers of observation.

Finally, as though waking from a dream, he asked, "What are you doing here?"

"What a daft question. I came to see you, of course."

"But how, I mean…"

"Miss Bird said you'd be up here—in your Highland retreat," she added tartly.

Rex made a mental note to throttle the housekeeper when he got back to Edinburgh.

"Och, don't look so cross," Moira said. "It's no her fault. I'm sure she just felt sorry for me after you jilted me so cruelly."

"Jilted? You ran off with that photographer in Baghdad!"

"I tried to apologize. I even went all the way to Florida to see you."

"Aye, well I'm not looking for a repeat performance." *What on earth did she hope to achieve by turning up here?* he asked himself.

"I wasna well in the spring. I was still traumatized by the bombing, but I'm better now and I want to try again. I'm sorry aboot what I put you through." Moira shivered. "Will ye no let me in out of the rain?"

"This is right awkward," he told her, moving aside so she could pass into the hall. "Helen's here."

"You're still with her?"

"I bought this place for the two of us."

"I see. Well, it's high time I met my rival, don't you think? Don't worry—I'll be all sweetness and light. Who else is here? I saw a van, a Land Rover, and a couple of other vehicles in the driveway."

Standing with Moira under the light from the teardrop chandelier, Rex noticed that she had made up her face. This came as a surprise since Moira, a self-professed feminist, had eschewed such tactics to attract men in the past. And she wore what he took to be an expensive perfume.

"What happened to your lift?" he asked, recalling the departing taillights.

"I came by taxi. I sent it away once I saw you were home."

"You came all the way from Edinburgh in a taxi?"

"I don't drive, remember, and I didna expect you'd come and pick me up from the station in Spean Bridge, or if I'd find a cab service there. The driver almost couldna find this place. I suppose

I'll have to stay the night." She brushed her hand down her wet coat. "It's no weather to be oot looking for a hotel."

"The owners of the Loch Lochy Hotel are here. I'm sure they could put you up. That's their van outside."

"They'll never get out wi' that van. It'll get stuck in the mud. The cabbie almost refused to bring me down here. There's no sign of any letup. The rain'll only get worse."

Rex slowly banged the back of his head against the wall. "You'll have to promise to leave first thing in the morning."

"Now, now, Rex," Moira said. "Don't let's start all that again. Remember what happened last time."

"Rex?" Helen's voice came at him from down the hall. "Is everything okay?"

"Helen, meet Moira."

"Nice to make your acquaintance, Helen," Moira said sweetly, as promised, holding out her hand. "Sorry I'm late. There was an accident on the M90 and traffic was backed up for miles."

"Oh, I didn't know we were expecting you," Helen faltered, taking the proffered hand. She stood a couple of inches taller than Moira, who gazed up at her with calculating eyes.

"It must have slipped Rex's mind." Moira skirted around Helen and made toward the sounds of voices and music emanating from the living room.

Rex listened in trepidation.

"Hello, everyone, I'm Moira, an old flame of Rex's. Oh, what a lovely spread. I'm starving! And I could do wi' a drink. The roads are a nightmare what wi' all this rain …"

Rex knew from experience that Moira and drink did not mix well. The daughter of an alcoholic, she was a lifetime teetotaler before she went to Iraq. Rex had first seen her drink in Florida. The result had been disastrous.

"Rex?" Helen asked beside him. "What's going on?"

He jammed his hands into the pockets of his corduroys. "I have no idea, except that the housekeeper told her I was here."

"Is she sane?"

"Who? Miss Bird? Apparently not."

"No—*Moira*. Is she still under psychiatric care?"

"I don't know. I haven't seen her in months. In fact, no one has. She no longer attends the church meetings. The Charitable Ladies of Morningside were trying to get her interested in social work again, but … Oh, I suppose I should have visited her to see how she was getting on." Rex slumped against the wall.

"She seems a bit hyper," Helen said. "Her eyes are glittery. Not a good sign."

Laughter spilled from the living room as the voices grew more animated.

"What do you think we should do?" he asked Helen.

"Better try not to antagonize her. Don't show me any affection."

"Helen, I'm so sorry. This was supposed to be a special weekend for us."

"There will be other weekends. We should attend to the guests." With a wintry face, Helen moved off toward the living room.

Rex glanced at his watch. It was only nine-thirty. The rest of the night would be murder. He would have to keep a careful eye on Moira and hope the situation did not blow up in front of his guests. Not that he really cared what they thought. Alistair, the only one who counted as a friend, would understand. However, he didn't want to embarrass Helen. She had worked so hard in preparation for this party.

By the time he returned to the living room, Moira had a small entourage gathered around her, with all but the two youngest guests in attendance. Flora was watching the group from across the room while Donnie tried to puzzle out one of Rex's multicolored Rubik's Cubes.

Alistair handed Moira a glass of white wine. The woolly haired Estelle plied her with food from the table. Cuthbert sat on a footstool at her feet, listening to her recount the perils of her journey. The Allerdice couple and Rob Roy Beardsley had pulled up chairs and were all ears.

"You poor dear!" Estelle exclaimed when Moira told her audience how she had witnessed a head-on collision and seen bodies pulled from the wreckage.

"It was just like the car bombing at the market in Baghdad, only I wasn't just a spectator that time—I was actually buried under a pile of rubble. An Australian photographer saved my life."

"You should write a book about your experiences in Iraq," Beardsley suggested.

"Perhaps I should." Moira's sharp brown eyes lingered on his face. "Do I know you from somewhere? You look familiar."

The journalist looked abashed. "Och, I'm no famous yet."

"Oh, well. You have a Glaswegian accent, so maybe we passed in the street years ago when I lived there. I've met so many people on my travels."

"It was very brave of you to go to Iraq," Shona Allerdice cooed in admiration.

"What were you doing out there?" Alistair asked, sitting forward in his chair.

"I went to help the Iraqi civilians. Our relief unit provided everything from food and uncontaminated drinking water to blankets and medical supplies. We equipped schools with the basics so the bairns could get on with their studies…"

Turning away, Helen raised an eyebrow at Rex. "She's got them eating out of her hand," she murmured.

"Aye, she can be very dramatic when it suits her."

"She's prettier than I imagined," Helen said grudgingly. "You never told me she had such nice hair."

"Och, I'd hardly call her pretty. You're pretty. But she can look attractive enough when she's in her element."

"Well, she's in her element now. Just look at Hamish and Cuthbert fawning all over her."

"And Alistair, poor fool. I should warn him."

Helen stared at Rex in amazement. "What do you mean? He's gay! You can't tell?"

"Really? Are you sure?" Rex trusted Helen's intuition about these things. She was invariably right.

"Pretty certain," she said.

Rex searched his memory. "That would explain why I've never seen him with a woman in all the years I've known him. He must be a closet gay. I've never seen any indication…" He thought for a moment. "Wait a minute. He did stay at the Loch Lochy Hotel with the young solicitor who did the conveyancing for the lodge. I wonder…I thought it strange they should both be staying up here. Most solicitors rarely venture out of their offices for their work."

"There you are, then," Helen told him. "So, where are we going to put Moira? I'm assuming she's spending the night. I didn't see a car."

"She came by taxi. We'll have to put her in the room with the leaky radiator, unless she can go with the Allerdices back to their hotel."

"Wouldn't that be nice."

"If push comes to shove, Alistair could take the sofa in the library and she could have his room."

"Oh, let her have the leaky radiator," Helen decided. "I just hope the Allerdice crowd don't have to stay over as well. The rain is coming down thick and fast."

It could be heard pummeling the eaves and drilling into the expanse of lawn. It washed in waves down the living room windows. Rex was glad he had installed double glazing on this side of the house. There were enough leaks already.

Moira had removed her coat and wore a becoming pale blue silk dress that draped her child-like frame.

"I need a drink," Helen said, making a beeline for the cabinet.

Rex crossed over to the window seat to see how the young Allerdice siblings were doing. "Why so glum?" he asked Flora. "Are you not enjoying the party?"

She smiled weakly. "Your friend seems to be having fun," she said with a nod in Moira's direction, where Alistair was topping up her wine glass.

"I didn't know she was coming. Did either of you want some sponge cake?"

"Aye, ta verra much," the boy replied.

"I'll get you some," his sister told him, hopping off her perch.

Donnie beamed after her.

"Your sister takes good care of you."

"That she does."

"I see you figured out the Rubik. Well done, it's the hardest one in my collection. It takes most people a lot longer."

"Flora helped me—just a wee bit."

Rex followed Donnie's cross-eyed gaze to Moira, who was now absorbed in a conversation with Alistair by the window where the rain played a staccato accompaniment, drowning out their words. Her brown eyes held the seductiveness of smooth milk chocolate. She held her painted lips slightly parted in rapture at what he was saying.

Since when had she turned into such a Jezebel? Rex wondered. One thing was for sure—she was not the same woman since she had returned from Iraq. Did she know Alistair was gay? Moira could be a little naïve, as demonstrated when she had run off with the married photographer, who had subsequently returned to his wife in Sydney.

Rex looked around the room to see if anybody's glass needed a refill. Allerdice and Farquharson were discussing hunting and how many kills they each had to their credit. Their wives were helping Helen clear the table. Rex wandered off to the front porch to smoke his pipe.

The rain fell in oblique sheets, isolating the lodge from the outside world. He lit the bowl of his pipe, filled with mellowy fragrant Clan tobacco, and stood leaning against the wall of the house, enjoying the fresh moisture-laden air.

The potholes in the driveway had filled to capacity. The road leading up to the village must have turned into a mudslide by now.

A four-wheel drive might still manage to get up there, but the hotel van? Not a chance, he decided.

He began to resign himself to the fact that he would have a full house that night. The Farquharsons had the main guest room next to his on the side overlooking the loch. Moira could take Alistair's room and possibly share with Flora. The Allerdice couple, if they had to stay over, could occupy the room with the leaky radiator at the top of the stairs. That left Rob Roy Beardsley and Donnie. There was a serviceable sofa in the living room for the journalist and a trundle bed in the stable equipped with blankets where the boy could sleep if he wished to stay with his pony. One or other of the McCallum brothers had slept there on occasion while work was progressing on the house.

Rex puffed on his pipe with satisfaction at having sorted out the logistics of the situation. There would be plenty for the guests to eat at breakfast. The only inconvenience, Rex supposed, might be the lack of bathrooms. He and Helen had one off their bedroom. A full guest bath with a ball-and-claw-footed Victorian tub occupied the upper landing. A cloakroom—or as the interior decorator had pretentiously described it, a "powder room"—was located downstairs off the hall.

Savoring the last of his pipe, he tapped the contents from the bowl into a flowerbed, with a final wish that all the guests could go home so he and Helen could salvage some time to themselves. When he returned inside, he found the center of the living room emptied of furniture.

"We're having a *ceilidh*," Shona Allerdice whispered to him conspiratorially.

Rex didn't see the need for all the secrecy, until he saw her slide a surreptitious look in her daughter's direction. Flora stood in a corner with her brother in apparent nervous anticipation.

"What sort of music would you like for the dance?" Rex asked Shona.

"Oh, I looked through your CDs and found some compilations of traditional Scottish tunes that'll do grand."

Rex, who had two left feet, would have preferred some other form of entertainment, but Shona was obviously not to be deterred. The others sat expectantly on the pushed back burgundy velvet chairs and matching sofas, clasping glasses of wine and whisky.

"All Shona's idea," Helen murmured, moving close to him as the lady in question busied herself with the stereo system. "The wine must have emboldened her."

"Blast the woman."

"Yes, I know how much you hate dancing."

"She could have consulted with me first."

"She seems to have some scheme up her sleeve. Don't look so put out, Rex. The party is a raving success."

"They're all staying, I suppose?"

"Alas, yes. Shona asked me if it would be an imposition. What could I say? It's still pouring outside and, in any case, I don't think we could find one designated driver among them. The Scots drink like fishes."

"Och, well, we might as well make the most of it." Rex looked around the room. "Where's Moira?"

"She said something about Alistair being kind enough to give up his room, and he went to help her with her suitcase. Looks like she planned on staying for at least a few days."

"Over my dead body."

"Here they are now."

Moira and Alistair entered the room, looking pleased with themselves. Moira went to the stereo to consult with Shona on the music. "The Gay Gordons, followed by some softer music for slow dancing," she suggested.

Shona concurred with a gleam in her eyes. "So how long were you with Rex?" she asked, loud enough for everyone to hear.

"A few years. Right up until I went to Baghdad, in fact. I was heartbroken to find when I returned that he had met someone else."

Rex itched to set the record straight, but good manners prevailed. He would just have to withstand the withering gazes branding him a cad.

"Well, I imagine you and Rob Roy must have a lot in common," Shona said, dragging Moira toward the journalist. "You're both well travelled. And both from Glasgow, I heard."

"She's a right Mrs. Bennet, isn't she?" Helen whispered in Rex's ear. "She'll have all the single women married off by the end of the evening."

"One in particular, I'll be bound—if she could." He cocked his head in Flora's direction.

Helen shook her head slowly and sighed. "It's pathetic the way her poor daughter looks at Alistair."

"He is a catch. A handsome advocate from a rich family—what more could a mother like Shona wish for?"

"Perhaps we should set her straight, so to speak."

"Och, let's not meddle. I hate gossip and silliness."

"You're right. We'll just see how it all plays out."

Shona Allerdice pressed the button on the CD remote and a burst of bagpipes issued forth.

"Let the games begin," Rex muttered under his breath.

FIVE

"GRAB YOUR PARTNERS," SHONA announced, pushing Flora at Alistair.

Moira and Rob Roy, who had no choice but to dance together since they were standing side by side, joined Flora and Alistair on the cleared floor. Estelle and Cuthbert fell into step, followed by the Allerdice couple and then Helen and Rex.

"Watch your feet," he warned as they marched backward four steps.

"I must say, the Gay Gordons is a bit of an irony," she remarked, glancing meaningfully over at Alistair and Flora, whose mother kept watch on the couple over her husband's shoulder.

"Maybe you're wrong aboot him," Rex suggested.

"I don't think so."

"Fabulous party," Estelle called out, baring her long teeth. "I could dance all night!" And off she galloped with Cuthbert, who was perspiring all over his red face.

"Yes, jolly good show," he wheezed in Rex's direction.

"We really should do this more often," Shona added, arms entwined with her husband's. "After all, we're only a stone's throw away!"

Helen grinned at Rex's discomfiture. "That's what you get for throwing such good shindigs."

"It's your fault. Your cooking is irresistible, as are you."

His attention was suddenly diverted by a commotion across the room. Donnie, who had been horsing around on the dance floor, had accidentally tumbled into Rob Roy Beardsley and sent him tripping headlong across the rug. The journalist's spectacles flew off and, retrieving them, the boy tried them on and grinned.

Rob Roy snatched them off the boy and whisked them back on his nose. "You wee imp! They're the only pair I have."

"He didna mean any harm," Flora intervened, taking her brother's arm.

"He should watch where he's going." Beardsley's normally pale face had turned scarlet. "He could cause someone harm, charging about like a bull in a china shop."

"Och, save yer breath to cool yer porridge, Rob," the boy's father told him. "Donnie just gets a wee bit spirited at times, but he's harmless as a newborn lamb."

"Why don't you come and sit down." Shona prodded her son toward a sofa, but he shrugged her off.

"I'll go check on Honey," he said sulkily with a black look at Beardsley.

When the boy left, the dancing resumed, good humor restored.

"Rex, I bag the next dance," Moira declared breathlessly as Rob Roy twirled her beneath his finger.

"Och, you know I'm not one for dancing."

41

"The next one's a slow waltz. I'll lead you." She and her partner joined hands in a ballroom hold and skipped away in a polka around the room.

Rex sighed miserably.

"Don't worry on my account," Helen said. "If she tries anything on, I'll slit her throat with the cake slicer. And you're doing quite well, by the way. My toes are still intact."

"That's because my mind's elsewhere. If I think too hard aboot where I'm placing my feet, I trip over them."

"Are you thinking about me?"

"Aye. I'm thinking how lovely you look tonight with that pink flush in your cheeks."

"Ha! This is a strenuous dance. That's why I'm flushed."

When it came to an end, everyone stood in place and clapped. A slower piece ensued, and Moira claimed Rex. Helen found herself with Rob Roy.

Moira's head barely reached Rex's shoulder. He lightly touched the small of her back and took her hand.

"I like your new place," she said.

"Thank you."

"Helen is a very lucky woman."

There was no tactful answer to this, and so Rex kept quiet.

"I won't cause any trouble," Moira said gravely. "There are plenty more fish in the sea."

"Many," Rex agreed. "And much fancier ones. Why settle for a minnow when you could catch a trout?"

"Do you consider Alistair a trout?"

"Aye, a rainbow trout. He comes from a very wealthy family and has impeccable credentials."

"He lost the MacClure case," Moira pointed out. "You'd have won it."

"Och, there's no guarantee. The prosecution had very little to go on."

"That poor wee lass. Imagine being left to die out on the moor, alone wi' her teddy bear."

Rex stopped in mid stride. "Och, I wish you hadna brought it up. It's right depressing."

"I can't stop thinking aboot it. She's the third bairn the police have found. There might be others. Dozens of children have been reported missing in the Highlands over the years. Some bodies will never be recovered, especially on Rannoch Moor. It's a wilderness of crag and peat bog, and no road for miles around in most places. What if the perpetrator is never caught?"

"We'll just have to pray that he is. Parents will have to be more vigilant."

Alistair came up to ask Moira for the next dance. He winked at Rex over her head, and Rex understood that he was thoughtfully taking her off his hands for Helen's sake.

"Cheer up, Rex," she said, approaching. "You actually look depressed that Moira's dancing with another man."

"It's no that. It's just that she brought up the murder of Kirsty MacClure. Did you hear about it in England?"

"Of course. It was all over the news. That blond child with the angelic face? It was heartbreaking."

Rex hugged Helen to him and kissed the top of her head. "I'll go make coffee for the guests."

"Good idea. I'll give you a hand."

After coffee was served along with a tray of liqueur chocolates, Rex went to dig up some extra sheets and blankets. The Allerdice couple would have to put up with the leaking radiator, since Alistair had relinquished his room to Moira.

Beneath the shelter of a huge golf umbrella, he took an armful of bedding out to the stable, where he found Donnie already asleep on the trundle bed, and covered the boy with a woolen rug. In a nearby stall, the Shetland pony snuffled contentedly, her nose buried inside a bucket of oats. Rain lashed the stone building, but in here reigned a reassuring aroma of dry hay and old leather. A cast-iron Victorian conservatory heater emitted radiant warmth from its coals. Satisfied that the boy was comfortably settled in for the night, Rex tiptoed out of the stable and charged back through the deluge.

At the house, the party was breaking up, the guests yawning and stretching. Estelle was searching for her shoes, which she had discarded for the dancing. Cuthbert mopped his brow with a paper napkin.

"Donnie is dead to the world. It's warm and dry in the stable," Rex assured the boy's parents. "And there's a bit of light from the heater."

"We're sorry to put you out like this," Shona apologized.

"Not at all."

"If we stay much longer, we'll eat you out of house and home. That was a delicious buffet, Helen."

"Aye," Hamish agreed. "Fancy a job at the hotel?"

Helen beamed. "I'm glad you enjoyed it as much as I enjoyed preparing it—in Rex's fantastic new kitchen." She put an arm around his waist.

"Well, we had better let these two lovebirds get to bed," Hamish said in a suggestive way that Rex did not appreciate in the least.

"Aye, well there's some tidying up to do first," his wife replied.

"Oh, leave that, Shona," Helen insisted as Mrs. Allerdice stacked the cups and saucers. "I'll see to it."

"Och, nonsense. I'm used to it."

Moira announced she wanted to take a bath and effusively bid everyone good night, saying she needed her beauty sleep.

"You're quite beautiful enough, my dear," Cuthbert said gallantly, taking her hand and kissing it. "Have you ever seen such tiny hands?" he asked his wife.

"You are incorrigible, Bertie. Just ignore him," Estelle told Moira. "That's what I do."

Rex offered the Farquharsons the use of his en-suite bathroom while he and Helen finished clearing up downstairs with Shona and Flora's help.

"Hopefully we'll make it back to the hotel before our guests get up," Mrs. Allerdice remarked. "We only have six of them, none of them particularly early risers, fortunately."

"Where did Hamish disappear to?" Rex asked her.

"I don't know. Do you need him?"

"Och, I can manage myself." He started to put the living room furniture back in its place. Alistair had retired to the library.

"I'll give you a hand," Beardsley offered.

"Aye, thanks. Will you be okay on this sofa?"

"No problem. I'll just use this throw rug."

Rex hesitated. The throw rug was mohair, and he wasn't sure Helen would approve of anyone using it as a blanket. He decided to let it go. There were few enough blankets in the house.

As he went to check under the stairs for more pillows for the guests, he heard Hamish's voice on the upstairs landing.

"Off for a nice bath, then? Can I scrub your back for ye?"

A tinkle of laughter floated down the stairs. "What would your wife say?" Moira's voice responded.

Rex placed his foot on the first step and listened.

"Och, she'd never have to know."

Moira said primly, "I don't go for married men."

Since when? Rex asked himself. That Aussie photographer was married. Probably had three kids too!

"You dinna ken what you're missing," Hamish said. "We're desperate and easy to please."

"Ta, but no. Please remove your foot from the door so I can have my bath."

"Show me what's beneath your dressing gown and I'll leave you alone, I promise."

"Go away before I scream." Of a sudden, Moira sounded alarmed.

Rex was about to rush up the stairs when he heard, "Tsh, tsh, I didna mean no harm. There you go."

The bathroom door closed, followed by the click of the brass bolt. Heavy footsteps made their way across the landing. "Wee tease," he heard Hamish mutter. Rex ducked out of sight as his guest opened the bedroom door at the top of the stairs.

The door next to Rex's bedroom opened, followed by a knock on the bathroom door. Returning to his post, Rex strained to hear.

"I say, is everything all right, Moira?" Mr. Farquharson called out.

The bathroom door creaked open. "Aye, thanks, Cuthbert. Hamish Allerdice has had a wee bit too much to drink, but he went on his way."

"A filly like you should be married. A slip of a thing such as yourself needs the protection of a man. By Jove, you look barely twelve years old wrapped in that towel…"

"I appreciate your concern, but I can look after myself."

"I know, you were in Baghdad with bombs going off all over the place and all that. Hardly a fit place for a woman. Arabs take a different view of women, you know. If you were my daughter, I'd—"

"Mr. Farquharson," Moira said firmly, "there's a draught and I'm getting cold standing here. I'll see you in the morning."

"Eavesdropping?" asked a voice behind Rex.

Helen stood behind him with an unreadable expression on her face. How long had she been standing there? he wondered.

SIX

"Hamish was pestering Moira," Rex explained to Helen at the foot of the stairs. "Cuthbert's up there offering assistance."

"Why don't you go up and join the adoring throng?"

"I just wanted to make sure she was okay. She is, after all, a guest in our house."

"Our house," Helen repeated wonderingly.

"Aye, and whether we like it or not, Moira is, for now, a part of our lives."

Helen sighed in desperation. "Oh, I know that. It's just a bit unnerving when she pops up out of the blue. At least Clive has the good manners to stay away."

Clive was the mathematics teacher Helen had been dating before she and Rex met. She and Clive used to go skiing in Aviemore, a winter resort not far from Gleneagle. "Well, he still teaches at your school, as far as I know," Rex pointed out.

"As far as you know." Helen shook her head. "That says it all. If you were the least bit jealous, you *would* know. You would have asked."

"Why would I be jealous? You said you found him boring."

"I did not!" Helen exploded. "You just assumed he was boring because he teaches mathematics."

"And drinks micro brews. And presumably won't get on his bike without one of those stupid helmets that make cyclists look like aliens on wheels." Rex laughed—until he noticed Helen's angry expression, and realized he had gone too far.

Suddenly she dissolved into laughter too. "You're right. What a dweeb!"

No voices came from upstairs now. Rex draped an arm around Helen's shoulders and guided her down the hall. He went into the kitchen and set the dishwasher in motion. "Don't worry about the glasses," he told the Allerdice women. "I'll take care of them in the morning."

After locking the kitchen door to the outside, he bid them goodnight and climbed the stairs with Helen, glad to finally get to his bed.

She followed him into the room and shut the door. "It's past midnight. Should we set the alarm for tomorrow?"

Rex groaned. "I'm not getting up before seven. Fortunately, it's a solid old house so we shouldn't hear too much noise. In any case, I'm so tired I could sleep through anything."

He brushed his teeth and got into bed. A creaking floorboard and muffled voices reached him from next door, where Estelle and Cuthbert Farquharson were staying. He expected the wall would be thicker. He'd never had overnight guests before, other than

Helen. Then the old water radiator started clanging as though struck repeatedly with a tire iron. Rex bunched a pillow against his ear. Just as he closed his eyes and murmured good night to Helen, an urgent knock rapped at the door. He thought about ignoring it.

"Rex!" Alistair's voice reached him in a fierce whisper. "Are you awake?"

With a deep groan, Rex threw off the covers and went to open the door in his pajamas. Alistair was still dressed in his suit. Closing the door, Rex stood with his colleague on the landing.

"What's the matter?"

"I turned on the late night news in the library," Alistair recounted, his face strained and shadowed in the light from the hanging lamp. "It's happened again." His words broke off in a strangled choke.

"What has?"

"There's been another Moor Murder!"

"A child?"

"A seven-year-old girl from Muiredge."

With a quick glance at the four closed bedroom doors, Rex led Alistair back downstairs. He did not want to upset his guests and worse, have them all get up again. However, Shona was still about, he saw with surprise. She looked up from the front door, where she appeared to be hiding something in her coat.

"All right, hen?" Rex asked, using a Scottish endearment reserved for women.

"I was just getting a bit o' air to clear my head. I had a wee bit too much to drink tonight," she added with an artificial laugh.

What an odd creature Shona Allerdice is, Rex thought. Yet he was too concerned with his friend to pay her much mind. Once they were in the library, he splashed whisky into two tumblers. The television, housed in an armoire with retractable doors, was set on low volume. Alistair stared at the screen as the clean-cut news anchor reiterated the details of the case.

"Melissa Bates was abducted from her cottage late this afternoon," he relayed in somber tones. "She was in the care of a babysitter, nineteen-year-old Gail Frith, who had left her playing in the front garden while she answered the phone. She did not report Melissa's disappearance immediately, hoping to find her before the parents got home. She knocked at the neighbours' doors. When a small boy mentioned seeing a green van with no windows in the back driving slowly down the road, Gail alerted the police. The surrounding moor was scoured for three hours before a police dog led authorities to an isolated spot seven miles from Muiredge. The girl's body was dredged from a bog near Loch Laidon. Heavy rain has impeded further investigation for the time being. If anyone has seen a green van in the area…"

Rex muted the volume. Alistair continued to gaze at the screen.

"This is my fault," he said, loosening his cravat. "I feel sick. I'm going to find Collins." He made purposefully for the door.

Rex held him back. "The police will already have picked him up for questioning. They'll round up all the pedophiles in a fifty-mile radius. They'll widen the net if they have to. Nobody wants to catch this monster more than the Bill." Or the parents, Rex thought. "This may be the crime that gets him convicted."

"The rain will have washed away all the evidence. It's a miracle the police found the body."

"I imagine they gave the dog an item of the girl's clothing and the animal was able to track the scent in spite of the rain. That dog deserves a medal." Rex was aware he was waffling on, but he could see how devastated his colleague was that he had not been able to put Collins away—if indeed Collins was responsible for the murders. It was, granted, a huge coincidence that no abductions had been reported while he was in custody. "It's amazing they found the body at all. Seven miles is a lot of ground to cover in such a short time, considering the rugged terrain."

"The wee boy was able to give the direction in which the van took off. He was looking out his bedroom window, wondering if the rain would stop for his birthday tomorrow."

"Lucky break."

"Collins got a lucky break when I was called upon to prosecute him," Alistair said bitterly, swirling his Scotch. "I wish Britain would bring back the death penalty for child killers. Oh, God, if I could just get a hold of him, I'd wring his neck with my bare hands." He flexed his long, pale fingers, a look of pure hate disfiguring his handsome features.

"Same M.O. as the others?" Rex asked reluctantly, dreading the answer.

"They haven't released specifics yet. And they may not."

Certain details of the Kirsty MacClure case had not been divulged to the press. Only the police and those involved in the trial knew about the means of strangulation and nature of the molestation. In the previous cases, other than ligature marks around the neck, no other evidence of physical trauma had been found, even though the victims had each been found stripped naked from the waist down. In the MacClure case, it had been determined that the little girl's elasticated undergarment had been used to asphyxiate her.

Rex wondered if an examination of Melissa Bates would reveal an escalation in the perpetrator's behavior.

"I tried calling Dalgerry," Alistair informed him. "But he's not answering his phone."

"He'll be busy with this new case. Just let the chief inspector do his job, Alistair. There's nothing you can do tonight."

"The poor parents!"

"The poor babysitter," Rex added. "Think how guilty she must feel. I wonder how long she was on the phone."

"She said only a few minutes, but she admits she was talking to her boyfriend, so who knows? Phone records will probably show it was twenty minutes or longer."

"I wonder what subterfuge the murderer used to lure the wee girl into his van. A kitten? Sweets? Oh, no," Rex exclaimed, noticing a water stain on the ceiling. "This place leaks like a sieve. Looks like it's coming from the guest bathroom." He tuned in again to the rain drumming on the eaves beyond the drawn curtains. "Now I'll have to get the roof looked at. It's like pouring money into a bottomless well."

"Didn't you get an inspection done?" Alistair asked in self-defense. He was, after all, the one who had notified Rex of the sale of Gleneagle Lodge and highly recommended the solicitor.

"I did, and there was a lot of deferred maintenance on the place which I was made aware of. I just did not expect everything to go wrong the moment I signed the papers. It should have been called The Money Pit." Rex shrugged helplessly. "And it needs to be properly winterized before I can use it for skiing holidays."

"It's a great investment," Alistair insisted. "You have all these acres and your own loch, for goodness sake."

"Aye," Rex conceded. "I like the place just fine. It's a great place for nature-walking."

"And skiing, eventually. Much better than paying those outrageous prices for lodgings in Aviemore."

"All right, you've convinced me, Alistair."

"I wish the little boy could have got a glimpse of the man," his colleague muttered, his attention reverting to the muted television set, which showed shots of rainy moorscape and an area of bog cordoned off with blue-and-white police tape.

"Wishes are futile," Rex cautioned Alistair. "Try to get some sleep. We'll call the police in the morning and see if there are any developments."

"I'll never be able to sleep." Alistair slumped into an armchair and put his head in his hands.

Rex went back upstairs to see if he could find a sleep aid. "I'm surprised you're still awake," he said, seeing Helen sitting up in bed reading a paperback novel.

Covering her mouth, she yawned deeply. "I was waiting for you. You've been gone twenty minutes."

"Won't be long now."

"What are you looking for?" she asked when he came back out of the bathroom. "I heard you ransacking the cabinet."

"Alistair needs something to help him sleep."

"Is he okay?"

"Aye, he's just a bit uptight about work."

"In my wash bag. I always travel with a few pills."

"Thanks, lass." Rex returned with the bag and sank down on the bed. He felt bad about lying to Helen, even if it was only by omission. The last time he had done that, it had almost cost him his relationship with her. But he didn't want to upset her with this new development.

He doubted he could sleep either after what he had seen on TV about the Melissa Bates murder. It made him glad his son, Campbell had reached age twenty without any serious mishaps in his young life. A broken toe and the removal of his tonsils was all. It also made him hesitant about seriously considering the possibility of having another child. Helen was still of child-bearing age and had mentioned a couple of times how she had always wanted a daughter. In light of the Moor murders, the prospect sent a shudder through his core.

"Rex?" Helen held out a couple of tablets in the palm of her hand.

"Aye?"

"You seem very pensive."

"I was having one of those philosophical moments when you weigh life's pleasures with the reality of the world we live in."

"You think too much."

"There's been another child abduction out on Rannoch Moor," he confided at last. "Alistair saw it on the news tonight. The police have recovered the body."

Helen clutched at the neck of her negligee. "Oh, my God! Poor Alistair. Is that why he can't sleep? Does he know the child?"

"No, but he was the prosecutor in the Collins trial. He thinks if he'd done a better job and got a guilty verdict, he could have prevented this latest murder."

"But Collins was acquitted because he had a watertight alibi for the exact time of Kirsty's death."

"Exact time of death can be very hard to pinpoint," Rex told her. "And Collins' girlfriend could have been lying for him, credible as she was on the witness stand. I just don't know. All I do know is that Alistair is a damn fine advocate and, if he doesn't get a grip on himself, it'll ultimately cost him his career. I've seen it happen before when barristers lose their nerve."

"Not every barrister wins practically every case. You're just exceptional."

Rex deposited a light kiss on her nose. "Thank you."

"Shall I make Alistair some warm milk to wash down these tablets?"

"No, just stay where you are. I'll be back to prove that I'm exceptional in places other than court."

"Oh, right," Helen said with a broad smile. "Hurry back, then."

SEVEN

By the time Rex drifted blissfully into sleep, the house was quiet beneath the downpour. He woke up once in the night, staying alert long enough to register the fact that Helen was not beside him before falling back into a deep slumber. Later, as dull light began to seep in around the curtains, he felt her warmth in the bed and thought how lovely it would be not to have to get up before some decadent hour of the morning. Nine o'clock would be heaven.

As he half rose from the pillows to peer at the luminous hands on the alarm clock, he became aware of an incipient headache, which he attributed to the whisky he had consumed the night before, and which he might have been able to sleep off given half a chance. As it was, the house was already alive with the sounds of people rising and preparing for the day.

At just after seven, as he was shuffling out of the bedroom in his slippers to see to his guests, Flora accosted him on the landing. "Do you mind if I use your bathroom? Someone's in the cloakroom downstairs and I've not been able to get into the one upstairs since yesterday night."

"Maybe the door's jammed." Rex tried the knob on the bathroom door. "It's locked." He knocked. "Hello? Is anybody in there?"

Flora, standing beside him with her thighs squeezed together, wore a pained look on her face.

"By all means, use ours," he told her. "Helen went down to the kitchen."

The young woman scooted into his bedroom. He knocked again at the bathroom door.

"What time does the paper arrive?" Cuthbert asked, emerging from his room.

"The boy usually delivers the papers before six."

"No sign of them, old chap. I've already been down. Maybe he couldn't get here because of the rain, though it's eased off a bit now."

"He comes on his bicycle, but he's never missed a delivery, even in snow."

Hamish Allerdice came out of his room, bleary-eyed and unshaven. "Morning," he croaked. He rattled the bathroom doorknob and swore. "Someone's in there. I haven't been able to get in all night. Had to go downstairs."

"Flora said the same thing," Rex informed him. "I really don't want to break down the door. Perhaps it locked itself. I'll go and see if I can get in through the window."

He mooched down the stairs and changed into his Wellingtons. Voices burbled from the kitchen. The faucet was running in the cloakroom. He imagined everyone must be up by now. Stepping outside the front door, he was struck by the penetrating chill.

A dreary rain persisted through the wan early morning light. Mist decapitated the tops of the hills and floated in wreaths across the silvery loch. A shiver coursed through his body and soul.

Turning the corner of the lodge, he glanced up at the bathroom window. He suspected it was locked, since it was close to a drainpipe and therefore accessible to a determined burglar. Still, it was worth checking before he caused damage to the bathroom door.

He kept a ladder in the stable. Pulling the back of his sweater over his head, he made a run for it, splashing through the puddles in the gravel driveway and splattering mud on his jeans.

At the near end of the stable, Donnie lay cocooned in his blanket on the trundle bed, snoring peacefully. Coals glowed in the free-standing heater, generating a pleasant warmth within the confines of the white-washed walls. Careful not to wake the boy, Rex grabbed the ladder from where it stood beside the power lawn mower, scythe, and sundry other garden utensils at the opposite end and, hoisting it onto his shoulder, trudged back through the rain.

Extending it to its full length, he propped it against the wall of the house and climbed to the bathroom window above the library. To his great relief, he found the sash window unlocked and managed to push it open with ease. As he did so, he remembered that this window had been on the McCallums' to-do list. It had been jammed shut from hardened paint when he purchased the house. They must have unstuck it and forgotten to lock it afterward. What a pair of incompetent fools! He should have hired someone else.

The window aperture proved a tight squeeze for his stocky build, and he was only able to execute the maneuver by bumping his head and scraping his ribs on the wood frame. No window treatments had yet been installed, but no one could see in except on a ladder. He landed beside the empty bath and surveyed the water pooled over the tiled floor.

Och, don't say we have a big leak in the ceiling! he despaired. He was beginning to think he probably should have shopped around a bit more before letting Alistair persuade him what a great investment Gleneagle Lodge would be. At the time he hadn't known that Alistair and the solicitor were more than just friends…

He stepped across the sodden bath mat and made muddy prints to the door. As he unlocked it, he noticed a dressing gown in the form of an embroidered burgundy kaftan hanging from the brass hook. It looked like something Moira might have brought back from Baghdad. Why had she not worn it back to her room?

He examined the opened door. Helen was crossing the landing at that precise moment.

"I came to ask you what you wanted for brea—Rex! Just look at your muddy feet! What are you doing? Why is the window open? There's a dreadful draught."

"I had to climb in. The door was locked."

"It looks like there was a flood in here!"

"I know. I canna understand it. The walls and ceiling are dry as far as I can see. I thought there must be a leak."

"Perhaps the McCallums can take a look when they come to fix the radiator." She stood in the doorway in a fluffy blue sweater and jeans, surveying the scene. "I'll get a mop."

"Nay, lass. You just see to breakfast. I'll clean this mess up."

"Would you like some eggs? I set up a buffet in the dining room."

"Tea and a bacon sandwich would be grand. Any signs of departure yet?" he asked under his breath.

"The Allerdices and Cuthbert Farquharson are still at table. Rob Roy is making eyes at Flora, but she won't have any of it. Her own eyes are on the bigger prize, I suppose. Her brother hasn't come in yet. I haven't seen Moira or Estelle either."

"You mean to say, the Allerdices are showing no signs of leaving yet?" Rex's face fell.

"It's a testament to your wonderful hospitality, Rex," Helen joked with a crooked smile that never failed to win him over. "They said the hotel cook and the waiter will have breakfast under control at Loch Lochy."

"The guests will probably be relieved not to have that silly Shona fussing over them."

"Well! Someone got out of bed on the wrong side this morning! See you downstairs." Kissing him lightly on the cheek, Helen backed into the landing. Rex shut the bathroom window, still flummoxed about the locked door.

"Gracious! What happened in here?" Estelle asked, sliding on the wet floor in her slippers and grabbing onto the sink for support, almost wrenching it out of the floor. She wore a crimson velvet dressing gown with frilly lace trim down the buttoned front. Her hair was in curlers and a greenish-gray face mask covered all but her mouth and eye sockets. "Sorry, if I look a fright," she said, taking note of the shock that must have registered on his face.

"Ehm ... Not at all. I was just trying to fathom how so much water got on the floor."

"Well, clearly someone had a bath and water must have sloshed over the sides. Perhaps they slipped. Those old-fashioned tubs are less stable than the modern ones."

"I've never had any trouble with them," Rex countered, though judging by how she had almost uprooted the sink, he could see how she might manage to dislodge one. "In any case, where is the person now?" he asked in vexation. "The door was locked. The bathroom was empty. They couldn't just have vanished. Unless they went through the window, and why would they have done that? I managed to unbolt the door without any problem. It wasna stuck."

"It might have locked itself after the last person went out," Estelle suggested, studying it. "Though I don't see how..."

Rex gathered up the towels on the rack and furiously mopped up the tiled floor. If people couldn't be relied upon to take care of his property, he simply wouldn't invite them again.

"Perhaps you have a ghost," Estelle teased. "The Ghost of Gleneagle Lodge! But I wouldn't go telling Shona Allerdice about it. She'll have that journalist researching the story and then you'll get no peace." She cast a cautious glance behind her. "That woman will do anything for a bit of publicity. All that nonsense last night about a sea monster in their loch! I couldn't keep my face straight."

"Aye, and another one in Loch Lown, if Beardsley is to be believed." Rex straightened up from his floor-mopping and confronted anew the rather startling apparition of Estelle Farquharson. The clay mask was beginning to crack into tiny fissures. It was a wonder she managed to talk at all. "A first cousin to the Loch Ness Monster!" he scoffed.

"Well, it's good for business, don't you see? The Loch Lochy Hotel is a dreadful place. Cuthbert had indigestion on the two occasions we had dinner there. The venison tastes like shoe leather, and the grouse! And don't get me started on the décor! It's so pseudo. Not real deer heads at all. Fakes! The place is going under, and so Mr. and Mrs. Allerdice are banking on this whole Lizzie business to save them."

"I think you may be right, and you know how gullible people are. Och, well, I'll let you get on with your beauty preparations, Estelle. The floor is just aboot dry now, and you'll find clean towels in the airing cupboard."

Wellingtons in his hand, he picked his way across the landing to fetch a pair of socks from the master bedroom.

"Rex, old man!" an Etonian drawl called out as he started down the stairs. "Come and see this!"

By now, Rex just wanted his breakfast. He swore never again to invite anybody to the lodge. It seemed the only people you wanted to actually turn up, didn't—like the McCallum brothers—and the rest just couldn't be got rid of! To top it all, the voice calling him belonged to Cuthbert, and he had little patience for people of his sort. But what could he do? Half-heartedly he strolled into the main guest bedroom where Mr. Farquharson was beckoning him over to the window. The rain had slowed to a jaded drizzle, almost ready to give up, but not quite.

"What is it?" Rex asked his guest, whose jowls were positively quivering in excitement.

Cuthbert pointed to the far side of the loch. Three quarters of a mile away, Rex could perceive a dark blur in the ripples.

"Here, look through these binoculars. They're Estelle's. She uses them for bird-watching."

Rex had difficulty adjusting the focus. Finally, he made out a longish shape undulating just beneath the surface of the water. It had a sleek head and a thin body or tail.

Rob Roy Beardsley burst into the room. "Is it Bessie? I was at the loch taking photographs when I saw you at the window with the binoculars. Can I borrow them a minute?"

"It's hard to see through the mist and drizzle," Rex said, handing them over to the journalist. "The subject looks wavy. It could be some flotsam and jetsam from the rainstorm that got washed up on the islet. Perhaps a tree trunk."

"It appears to be moving," Beardsley said, peering through the glasses. "Mind if I take your row boat out on the loch?"

"Be my guest. The oars are kept in the stable."

"I saw some Wellingtons in the hallway that might fit. The banks of the loch will be like a mire after all this rain ... "

"In my bedroom. I just took them off." Rex glanced at Beardsley's feet. He was a much smaller man than himself. "You'll be walking around inside them."

"I'll manage with extra socks. Ta very much."

"Just don't get swallowed up by the monster."

"I'll go with you, Rob," Cuthbert said. "I have my galoshes. I'll take the rifle just in case, Rex, if I may."

With great reluctance, Rex retrieved it from the bedroom with the defective radiator. Equipped with footwear and protection, the two guests took off, as gleeful as two schoolboys on an outing to the zoo. Shaking his head in wry amusement, Rex traipsed after them down the stairs. He knocked at the library door and entered when he heard no response. Alistair sat in an armchair watching the news in the same clothes he had worn the day before. The bottle of Glenlivet stood empty on a side table.

"Och, you look like death warmed up," Rex remarked. The gray stubble on his friend's chin and the dark circles beneath his eyes aged him ten years. "Have you been up all night?"

"The police have a suspect for the Melissa Bates murder. They won't say who it is yet."

"That's grand news!"

"Leads have been pouring in. Crime officers have been working at the scene collecting samples from the bog."

Rex nodded pensively. "I've taken many a hike across Rannoch Moor. It's surprising how much flora and fauna exist in such a godforsaken place. I have a collection of wild flowers and bog myrtle somewhere. Helen tends to prefer more scenic routes, preferably close to a tea and souvenir shop." He smiled at the fond memories of their hikes together. It was truly fortuitous that they had long walks in common. It was one of the things that had inspired him to purchase a property in the heart of the Highlands.

"Rannoch Moor is not a very touristy place," Alistair agreed.

"So then," Rex said. "Sounds like the police have got off to a good start. Have you had breakfast?"

Alistair pulled a face. "I feel a bit hung over, to tell the truth. You must think me a terrible house guest. I should not impose any further on your hospitality."

"Och, nonsense. Please stay. At least, as long as the Farquharsons do. I could do with the moral support."

"Fair enough. What's the 'old boy' up to this morning?"

"He took his hunting rifle out on the loch with Rob Roy Beardsley. They're out chasing Bessie."

"What a pair of loons. We should take a video of them and stick it on YouTube."

"Rob Roy's got a verra sophisticated camera. Who knows? Maybe there really is a sea monster out there and he'll make a name for himself."

"I wouldn't put it past him to doctor the pictures." Alistair turned his gaze back to the television screen, which showed bleak moorland beneath a tearful sky.

"Did you get through to Chief Inspector Dalgerry?" Rex asked.

"I left about six messages. Nobody will tell me anything beyond what's reported on the news. The sergeant just said they were 'interviewing' a person of interest who had been seen in the area where a green van was spotted."

"Sounds promising."

"If you say so. He did divulge that the man in question is not Collins."

Hence the long face, Rex thought. His friend was convinced Collins was the murderer of the young moor victims.

Helen stuck her head around the door. "There you are, Rex. Your breakfast's waiting. Alistair, come and at least have a cup of tea."

Alistair heaved himself out of the armchair and the men joined Helen in the kitchen, where various used pans and skillets stood on the shiny red Aga.

"Looks like you fed an army," Rex remarked. "Where are they all?"

"Down by the loch."

Rex took his tea and bacon sandwich into the garden and walked down the wet flagstone path to the loch that was edged with bright yellow gorse bushes. The rain had stopped for the moment. A stunned group stood huddled on the muddy bank, their eyes fixed on the wooden boat as Rob Roy and Cuthbert rowed feverishly through the mist toward them. Surely they had not actually had a close encounter with Bessie?

"Will she be all right?" Shona cried out.

"She's not breathing," the journalist called back. "Call an ambulance!"

"An ambulance?" Rex asked in surprise. *Did you transport sea monsters in ambulances?* "What's wrong with her?"

Hamish Allerdice turned to face him. "It looks like your ex-girlfriend drowned in the loch."

"Moira?" Was this some kind of joke?

"She's in the boat. I'm verra sorry for your loss. We thought it was a sighting of Bessie, but it turned out to be …"

Rex waded into the water, straining to see. In the bottom of the boat lay the naked form of Moira wrapped in a tarpaulin, her limbs stiff and blue, her hair entangled with weeds, eyes staring and glassy. There could be no doubt she was dead.

Drowned, in his loch.

EIGHT

"I'm sorry, Rex," Cuthbert said, hopping out of the boat and securing the line to a rusty stake in the rocks. "Rob Roy performed CPR. I'd say she's been dead for hours."

The two men lifted the dripping body from the boat, careful to keep the tarpaulin in place around her torso. Slimy reeds clung to her pale arms and streaming dark hair. Shona emitted a horrified gasp and turned away from the body. Flora draped an arm around her mother's heaving shoulders. The rest of the group offered Rex their condolences.

Helen ran down to the bank. "Moira!" she exclaimed upon seeing the corpse. "What happened? What was she doing in the loch? Did she go for a swim?"

"In this weather?" Estelle said with a dismissive humph, restored to normality in a tartan skirt and a chunky ivory wool sweater. Rid of her clay mask and curlers, she looked almost human. "She'd have had to be out of her mind."

Rex and Helen exchanged a look. Moira had attempted suicide in the spring following her return from Iraq when she had gone to Florida to try to reconcile with Rex, who was visiting his son. The doctor at the hospital where she'd been admitted had said she was suffering from Post Traumatic Stress Disorder as a result of her bombing experience in Baghdad.

It appeared she had not fully recovered ...

"The only reason she didn't sink," Rob Roy explained as he and Cuthbert made toward the house with the body, "was that she got caught up in the reeds."

"Why would she have gone swimming, Rex?" Shona pleaded. "Is this something you would have expected of her?"

"She announced she was going to have a bath, remember?" Estelle told the group following the pallbearers. "That's why we asked to use your bathroom, Rex."

"That would explain why she had no clothes on," Hamish remarked, barely able to disguise his prurient interest. "But how did she end up in the loch?"

"If it were me, I'd go for a swim first," Shona pointed out with a shudder. "Then I'd have a bath to warm up. Doing it the other way round makes no sense."

Rex had to agree that nothing about Moira's apparent drowning made sense so far.

"When's the ambulance getting here?" Alistair asked, wiping the rain from his eyes. "Should we bring her into the house?"

"Let's take her into the stable," Cuthbert suggested. "All right with you, old man?" he asked Rex.

Rex nodded. He felt slightly superstitious about dead bodies in the house. In any case, the ambulance would be here soon. Rob

Roy and Cuthbert conveyed Moira to the stable, where Rex instructed them to set her down on the trundle bed.

Donnie, who had just risen and was straightening his clothes, stared at her as at a ghost. "Is she deed?" he asked in heavily accented Scottish.

"Aye, Donnie, she is. She's at peace." His sister took his hand. "Come away, now. I'll make you some breakfast. May I, Helen?"

"Of course. Make yourselves at home. There's some porridge in the pan and scrambled eggs. You just need to put some bread in the toaster."

On a certain level Rex found it peculiar that people should be discussing breakfast when a young woman lay dead before them. Moira was only thirty-seven. It had been a while since he'd had any deep feelings for her, but now as he gazed upon her chilled face he felt unutterably sorry.

"I suppose we should all stay until the police get here," Hamish murmured. "I'll call the hotel and tell them there's been an emergency."

"The police will want to ask everybody what they saw," Shona said morbidly. "Won't we have something to tell the guests tonight!"

Rex could tell Mrs. Allerdice was trying to put on a brave face, but she was visibly shaken.

"I didn't see anything," Estelle remarked. "I was quite merry last night from all the wine and sherry. As soon as my head touched the pillow, I slept like a lamb."

Or a sheep, Rex thought uncharitably. Oh, *why* had Moira come to Gleneagle Lodge? Why had any of them come?

"I recall she went upstairs to take her bath before the rest of us retired," Estelle added. "And that's all I'll be able to tell the police."

"Moira was right fond of baths," Rex reminisced.

Helen took his arm and led him away. "Don't blame yourself."

"Donnie left first," Beardsley corrected Estelle. "To go to the stable."

The group reconvened by the horse stalls where Rex had found the ladder.

"I tried the bathroom in the middle of the night," Shona said. "And couldn't get in."

"Flora and Hamish couldn't either," Rex confirmed. "I think Moira may have drowned in the bath. That would account for all the water on the floor. The excess water suggests someone drowned her."

"On purpose?" Shona asked, shocked.

"Is there any other way?" her husband asked impatiently.

"But the door was locked from the inside," Cuthbert said, scratching his ear. "I tried this morning. I didn't hear a peep."

"Seems no one did," Rex said, pacing the small storage area. "Someone lifted her through the window and then dumped her in the loch, maybe to make it look like an accident. The killer must have used the boat and pushed the body over the side, but instead of sinking, she was washed up on the wee island."

"Who could have done such a thing?" Shona asked, pulling at the cowl neck of her sweater.

"It had to have been someone at the house," her husband replied, eying the group standing in the stable.

"Not necessarily," Alistair pointed out. "It could have been a burglar who surprised her in the bath."

Rex held up his hand for silence. A detail had just occurred to him. "Someone emptied the bath, unless the plug got dislodged in the struggle and drained by itself. Unlikely, therefore, Moira drowned herself. She went up for her bath just before midnight," he restated. "The women cleared up. Then everybody got ready for bed." He would have to think about this somewhere quiet. "Rob Roy was helping me move the furniture back."

"But what about the locked door?" Estelle insisted. "How did the person get in?"

"Through the bathroom window, presumably—using the ladder from the stable. I don't think the window was locked."

"That would support my burglar theory," Alistair said.

"If someone used the ladder, how did they get it without waking Donnie?" Helen asked. "Or did they take it before? Perhaps we should ask him if he remembers hearing anyone enter in the night."

"Donnie sleeps like a log," Hamish Allerdice told her. "He'd no hear much with the rain falling hard on this tile roof."

"He did not hear me this morning," Rex confirmed.

"Can we be sure it wasn't a suicide?" Estelle Farquharson asked practically.

"It would be easier to explain to my guests," Shona jumped in. "A murder might scare them away."

"Moira packed enough clothes to stay for a few days," Helen pointed out. "I don't think she would have gone to the trouble if she had planned to take her own life."

"Perhaps she was jealous when she saw you and Rex together," Estelle suggested. "You make such a happy couple."

Did Estelle Farquharson always have to say what was on her mind? Rex wondered with irritation. "Most people are incapable of drowning themselves twice," he retorted.

"What happens now, old sport?" Cuthbert asked.

Rex rubbed at his eyes. He wished he could wake up again with none of this having happened. If wishes were fishes… "Let's all go back to the house and wait for the authorities there."

"I'll make some more coffee," Helen offered.

"Cuthbert," he said before Mr. Farquharson could leave. "Do you recall if Moira locked the bathroom door after you finished speaking with her?"

"I waited to make sure she did. Anyone could have walked in on her in her bath. And," he added *sotto voce*, jerking his head at Hamish, "I was worried that old goat might come back and bother her."

When the others had gone, Rex performed a quick examination of Moira's body to check for contusions and other signs of violence to her body. He found bruising on her right side and scratches on the top of her hand. Catching up with Estelle, he asked to borrow her Nikon and returned to take photographs of the corpse.

That done, he carefully recovered the body with the tarpaulin and closed the door to the stable. With a fluttery feeling in his stomach, he crossed the courtyard and entered the house. He wished the police would get here. Looking into a murder was different when you knew the victim well. He felt confused. He was pretty sure Moira had not drowned herself, but how could he be certain? She had tried suicide before. Perhaps he was denying the possibility because he would feel responsible if that were the case.

It was possible she had drowned accidentally. But what were the chances of that? She had not been drunk when she went up the stairs and had sounded in control when accosted by Hamish at the bathroom door and afterward, when she spoke to Cuthbert. Rex realized with a small shock that that was the last time he had heard her voice and would ever hear it again.

Perhaps she had taken pills before she got in the bath, maybe a sleep aid, and the combination of alcohol, medication, and warm water had caused her to fall asleep and slip under the surface... Then someone had found her and panicked, and thrown her in the loch. An unlikely scenario.

Unless Moira had let that person into the bathroom through the door and returned to the tub (equally unlikely), the intruder must have come in by the window. This meant the person was up to no good in the first place. Would a burglar not just have fled when he saw a drowned body?

There could be little doubt: Everything pointed to murder.

NINE

REX LIT A LOG fire in the living room, and everyone shed their outer layers of clothing and sat down in silence. Helen and Shona brought in a tray of coffee and biscuits. The Allerdice children sat in the window box they had occupied the day before and stared out at the fitful rain.

"I should go muck out the stable and give Honey her oats," Donnie announced finally, heading toward the doorway.

"Don't disturb the body," Rex cautioned.

"How can I disturb her?" the boy asked stupidly. "She's deed."

"Just don't move or touch her," Flora explained to her brother.

Hamish rose too. "I'll give the lad a hand."

"Well," Estelle Farquharson said when the Allerdice men had left. "I suppose we had better get to the bottom of this. No point in wasting time. Who can vouch for whom all night? Most of us shared rooms, so that might be a starting point. Rex?"

"Excuse me?"

"Let's start with you and go round the room. Were you and Helen together all night?"

"Aye … I believe so. At least, from the moment we went upstairs." Rex paused with his coffee cup halfway to his lips. "Och, wait a minute now … Alistair came up to the room to discuss a case he was troubled about, and I joined him in the library. That was after midnight. I went back upstairs to get him something. Then I went back to bed and stayed there until morning."

"I can confirm that," Helen said beside him on the sofa.

And that's when Rex remembered—he had woken up late in the night and Helen was not in bed. He dared not look at her. Oh, but surely she would not have caused Moira harm, even though his ex-girlfriend had been a threat to their happiness.

Estelle smoothed her red tartan skirt across her ample hips and crossed her thick ankles. She was built like a tank, certainly strong enough to have pushed Moira out the window, Rex considered. She addressed her husband. "Now you, Bertie. You too must account for your movements."

"Dammit, old girl," Cuthbert responded. "My mind's in a fog about last night. I remember drinking and dancing and so on. I suppose at some point I stumbled upstairs and fell into bed."

He had spoken to Moira upstairs, Rex remembered.

"You used Rex's bathroom first," Estelle reminded her husband. "We both did. Then we turned in. Alistair?"

"Let's see now. I knocked on Rex's door because I wanted to tell him about the latest Moor Murder, which I'd just caught on the telly. We sat in the library talking for a while. I slept in there. Mostly dosed, actually. I heard the panes rattling from the rain. It was so loud that the pills Rex went to fetch to help me sleep didn't work."

"Shona. Your turn, dear." Estelle turned toward Mrs. Allerdice with a schoolmarmish expression of encouragement.

"Well, I helped Helen and my daughter with the dishes. There was someone in the upstairs bathroom, so I used the one downstairs. I got up once in the night and found the bathroom on the upstairs landing still occupied. I do remember the radiator leaking all night with a steady drip-drip-drip, but it was sort of hypnotic. Hamish snored away like a donkey as usual."

Mr. Allerdice was not in the room to object to his wife's characterization. Rex thought she might not have felt so bold had he been there. And what had she been doing outside?

Estelle looked across at the journalist who was nursing a cup of coffee. "Rob Roy, if you please."

Rex watched as the man hunched forward in his armchair and frowned in concentration. "I helped Rex put the furniture back in its place after the dancing. When the women had finished taking the plates and glasses away, I made myself comfortable on the sofa and put the blanket over my head. I was awoken one time in the night by a loud thud outside. It seemed to come from ground level. I thought perhaps a tree had fallen in the storm."

"What time was this?" Rex asked, searching around in a drawer for a paper and pen.

"Not sure, but I'd not been asleep long."

"What direction did the sound come from?"

"Down the hall by the library."

"Flora, can you remember anything?" Estelle asked the girl in the window seat.

Rex contained his irritation at not being allowed to direct the line of questioning himself, but so far Estelle was doing a decent job of asking all the basics. He concentrated instead on noting the guests' reactions.

"Well, actually, I did see something," Flora stammered, looking up meekly at Mrs. Farquharson and then away through the window.

The people in the room stared at her expectantly. The pen in Rex's hand stood poised, waiting for the revelation that might solve Moira's murder.

"Go on, Flora," Estelle prompted. "What did you see?"

"Well, I could have dreamt it, I suppose." Flora brought her vague gaze to rest on Mrs. Farquharson. "It was really strange— and quite frightening."

"Well?" her mother asked, eyes wide as saucers.

"It was a bulky shape on the stairs, with a large, odd-shaped head or else really weird hair." Flora's hands fluttered around her own listless brown locks held back in an Alice in Wonderland headband. "Of course, it *was* a shadow I saw, so it could have been distorted."

"Was it going up or down the stairs?" Rex asked.

"I'm not sure." Flora chewed on her lip. "I just shrank back into my room and waited."

"What were you doing out of your room?" Estelle questioned.

"As I told Rex, I needed to … go."

"Did you see what time it was?" he asked.

"About twelve-thirty. I locked myself in the room. I was supposed to be sharing with Moira, but since she never turned up,

I assumed she was spending the night, ehm, elsewhere." A flush crept up the girl's neck as she stole a look at Alistair.

Rex made a note of the time. "Can you tell us anything else about this apparition on the stairs?"

"It—it was carrying a long knife."

Shona gasped. "A knife! My poor child. Why didn't you say something before?"

"A knife, eh?" Cuthbert echoed.

"Good God," said Alistair.

Rob Roy smirked and stroked his beard. "I think you were having a nightmare."

"It seemed very lifelike." Flora kneaded her hands together. "I feel foolish for bringing it up. I almost didn't."

"Not at all," Rex said. "At least we know your door was locked as of around twelve-thirty last night. Presumably Moira was dead by then or you would have heard her knock to get in. She wasn't with Alistair."

At around the time Flora claimed to have seen the Gorgonesque monster, he had brought the sleeping pill downstairs to Alistair. Or perhaps it had been a bit later. Either of them could be mistaken by ten minutes or so. He had not been aware of any movement in the communal areas of the house, but with so many people staying over, he had not paid much attention. On top of which, the house creaked like an old ship at sea, not to mention the din the radiators made when water gushed through the pipes.

Hamish returned from the stable. "No sign of the ambulance. We really need to get back to the hotel, Rex. Donnie has the pony bridled and is ready to set off. It's a five-mile hike through the glen."

"I'll call 9-9-9 again." Rex rose from the sofa and picked up the phone. "The line's dead," he said in surprise.

"Uh-oh," said Cuthbert.

"Could be from the storm," Hamish suggested. "Shona has her mobile with her."

"Yes, but I can't find it. I must have put it down somewhere last night. I looked for it this morning. I thought if the hotel called, I'd hear it and be able to locate it."

"Who called the ambulance earlier on?" Rex asked the people in the room.

"I did," Flora said.

"Can you call again, please."

She pulled the cell phone from her cardigan pocket and flipped it open. "The battery's flat. It's a terrible phone—never holds a charge."

"Who else has a mobile?"

"I do," Rob Roy said, "but it got soaked in the boat. It might start working again when it dries out."

"I object to the damn things," Cuthbert expostulated. "They should be banned from public places—"

"Shut up, Bertie," his wife interrupted. "We're discussing a murder. We're not interested in your peeves just now."

"Sorry, old thing." Cuthbert helped himself to a tumbler of whisky, even though it was only mid-morning.

"I didn't bring my mobile," Alistair apologized. "I decided to take a break for the weekend."

Rex sighed. "I left mine behind in Edinburgh too, for the same reason, but I'm sure Helen brought hers."

"I didn't, I'm afraid. I left it at home. I was already thirty miles from Derby when I remembered. It was too late to turn back."

That's wonderful, Rex thought. Ten people and not one working phone among them. "Perhaps Moira had one. I'll look in her bag."

"Good thinking, old chap," Cuthbert approved.

Rex crossed into the hall where a coat stand held the guests' outdoor apparel. A tapestry bag, which he recognized as Moira's, stood on the marble-top tripod table. He rifled through a bunch of keys, a packet of tissues, a couple of lipsticks, and a purse. Careless to leave it out in the hall with strangers about, he reflected. The previous evening when she arrived, she must have abandoned it there before going into the living room to meet his guests.

Perhaps he should check for the phone in the suitcase. He hurried upstairs to what had originally been designated as Alistair's room and where Flora had spent the night, and sifted through the clothes and toiletries in the leather case in what proved to be a futile exercise. It was bizarre that Moira had left Edinburgh for a place she had never visited before without taking her cell phone with her.

If she had brought a phone, someone must have taken it. That same someone could have stolen Shona's phone. There was nothing for it but to drive to the village and alert the authorities from there.

"Can I borrow your Land Rover?" he asked the Farquharsons upon returning to the living room. "I'll never be able to drive up the hill in my car after all this rain."

"Want me to come with you?" Cuthbert asked.

"I'd rather you stayed behind and held the fort."

On the spur of the moment, he had decided that Cuthbert, despite his predilection for shooting deer, was more of a known quantity than the other men. Hamish could not be accounted for after he had gone to bed, nor Alistair, for that matter. The two youngest men, Rob Roy Beardsley and Donnie, he knew least of all.

Plus, Cuthbert did not look like he had the strength to force a dead weight through the window, even a wee thing like Moira. As for the women, Rex could not be sure…

He hoped he was right about Cuthbert; Cuthbert had the rifle. Under the circumstances, Rex could not confiscate it.

"Right-oh," Mr. Farquharson said self-importantly, tossing Rex the keys to the Land Rover.

"Alistair," Rex began, leading his colleague out of earshot. "Can you keep an eye on the body?"

"No problem. I'll get my jacket."

Rex turned back to the group. "Please, all of you, stay in the house. Make yourselves comfortable. I won't be long."

"I'll come with you," Helen said, jumping up from the sofa. "You weren't thinking of leaving me alone with this lot, were you?" she asked as they pulled on their anoraks and Wellington boots in the hall.

"Nay, lass."

"I can't wait to get away. You can just feel the tension in the house. Shona and Hamish had a huge big row this morning, going at it like hammer and tongs—"

"What were they arguing about?" Rex cut in.

"They were in their room. I only heard raised voices and Hamish calling her a stupid cow."

"Charming." But then Shona had been equally uncompliment-ary about her husband's snoring. He led Helen outside by the arm. "Look, there's something we need to clear up."

"What about?"

"Last night I woke up to find you weren't in bed."

"I must have been in the bathroom. I couldn't sleep, so I thought I'd take one of the pills I gave you for Alistair."

"Why couldn't you sleep?"

"I don't know…I was tossing and turning, worrying about Moira."

"What do you mean?"

"She was trying so hard to win you back."

They stood under the stone porch watching the rain, which had redoubled its assault.

"She seemed quite taken by Alistair, I thought." Rex flipped his hood over his head in preparation for the dash to the Land Rover.

"You are such a modest fool, Rex. She was trying to make you jealous by singling out the most eligible bachelor in the house. That's why she so brazenly flirted with him."

"Oh—I see."

"Really, Rex," Helen said almost crossly. "For someone so intel-ligent, you can be truly dense at times." She tucked her blond hair inside her hood. "Come on. Let's go."

They ran across the driveway to the white Land Rover. At that moment, Alistair approached them. "Look here," he murmured, rain trickling down his lean features. "Moira's body has been in-terfered with."

"What do you mean?" Rex demanded.

"The tarpaulin has been moved."

"Is she exposed?"

"Not exactly. It's as though someone took a peek and hurriedly covered her up again."

"The boy might have taken a look," Helen said. "It's only natural at his age."

"That's what I thought," Alistair concurred. "And he's not quite right in the head."

"My bet is equally on the dad," Rex told them. "He has a reputation for being overly fond of the ladies." Hamish had stared inappropriately at Helen the previous evening, as he remembered with distaste.

"Not surprising, considering the mousy thing he's married to."

"Alistair!" Helen chided.

"Well, what do I know?" Alistair gave a graceful shrug, the shoulders of his gray jacket growing darker beneath the deluge. He stuck his hands in his pocket. "I'm gay," he added. "In case you hadn't guessed."

"I had."

"Alistair, please see to it no one else is disrespectful to Moira's body," Rex implored him. "I should not have let Donnie go back in the stable, but I thought it would be okay if his dad was there too. If I had time, I'd knock Hamish's block off, even if just for not teaching his son better manners. Look, we best be heading off," he told Helen.

"We can't," she said roundly.

"How not?"

"Slashed tyres."

"Good God, she's right," Alistair exclaimed, walking around all the vehicles. "Every single one."

TEN

WHEN REX SAW THE vandalized tyres, he felt ready to bellow and stomp his feet.

"Rex, I'm frightened," Helen said in a small voice beside him.

"Don't worry, lass. We'll get out of here one way or the other. Where's that boy?"

Glancing about him, he strode off beyond the stable to the meadow, where Donnie stood beside Honey as she grazed peaceably beneath the rain. When the boy saw Rex, he led the pony by the reins through the wet grass toward him. Rex realized Honey was too small to be of any use to him after all.

"I don't suppose your horse would support my weight, would she?" he asked.

"Och, noo, and she's right mean-spirited," Donnie told him in his slow, deliberate way. "She'll throw you just as soon as look at you."

"She's looking at me now, and not kindly."

The pony regarded him with much of the white of her eye showing, while her hind quarters did a little stampede on the spot.

Donnie stroked the length of her furry neck. "She kens you'd squash her."

Rex was not willing to send the boy to the village on his behalf, even though he would get there quicker on horseback—if he ever got there at all. "Perhaps you should put Honey back in her stall," he told Donnie. "I think we may all be here for a while yet. And I don't want you catching a chill."

The boy obediently led the horse toward the stable. Rex saw the bone-handled sheath knife was still in his belt. Had he slashed the tyres when he cut the phone line? Rex dismissed the idea. The careful planning involved in the murder all but ruled out the mentally disabled boy as a suspect.

"Donnie," he called after him. "Did anyone borrow your knife?"

"No one," the boy answered slowly. "I always keep it on me. Da gave it to me for my seventeenth birthday and said not to lose it as it cost more than he could afford."

"Alistair," Rex said when he drew near his colleague. "Follow the lad. When he's seen to the pony, send him into the house. I'd rather they all stayed together."

"Are you walking to the village?"

"We have no choice. We'll try to get a lift back."

Rex took off up the road with Helen, avoiding the worst of the puddles and potholes. The gravel crunched soggily underfoot. The damp chill on his face and the gentle patter of rain on the hood of his anorak made for a dismal walk, aside from the sad nature of his errand.

Someone had murdered Moira under his roof. That was the most logical explanation for all the water on the bathroom floor. The question that haunted him was whether the killer was a guest at Gleneagle Lodge or else an intruder who had snuck into the house with more than robbery in mind.

Rex pondered this last possibility. There were two points of access to the lodge: the front entrance and the kitchen door; and, of course, an unlocked window. The downstairs had been all lit up. Anyone could have peered inside while the inhabitants were partying and crept in at some point, perhaps when they were all in their rooms. He remembered locking the kitchen door, but not the front door, in case Donnie needed to get in the house.

Moira was prone to taking long baths, but she would have had to have been inconsiderate in the extreme to voluntarily remain in the bath for hours when people were trying to get in to use the facilities.

And what about the shadow Flora had seen on the stairs at around twelve-thirty? The apparition with a distorted head and a long knife?

"A penny for your thoughts," Helen said, trudging breathlessly beside him. "Actually, I'd give a lot more to know exactly what goes on in your head sometimes."

"I'm just trying to sort out this whole mess. Did Moira seem suicidal to you last night?"

"Hardly. Quite the belle of the ball, I'd say, and enjoying every minute of it."

"You were the belle, Helen."

"If you say so."

Rex stopped in his tracks and turned Helen to face him. Her hood slipped into her eyes as she lifted her face to look up at him. He pulled it back tenderly. "She's dead, Helen."

"I know." Helen burst into soft tears. "I'm sorry."

"It's not your fault." He took her by the arm and together they crested the hill and started down the country road that led to Gleneagle Village. Droplets of rain detached from the branches of the overhanging trees and fell onto the grass, where clumps of bluebells drooped beneath their watery burden. Sodden leaves clung to their boots as they trudged along. Not one car passed on the winding strip of blacktop.

"This reminds me of when we escaped to the pub from Swanmere Manor," Helen told him. Snowbound at an English country hotel owned by a friend of his mother, they had skied down to the village to find the local constable and report a couple of suspicious deaths. "I must be a bad luck charm," she added miserably.

"Don't be daft, Helen. You were nowhere aboot when I had that case in the French West Indies, or in Florida, for that matter." He let out a heavy sigh. "It's a wee bit different when it's on your own turf."

"I was thinking … If Moira had had a bit too much to drink, she might have accidentally slipped in the bath and sloshed water all over the floor. Oh, wait," Helen said before Rex could interrupt her. "That doesn't explain how she ended up in the lake. But if she was drunk—I mean *really* drunk, she might have climbed out of the window and decided to take a swim. Then it wouldn't be a murder at all," she added hopefully.

"Does that seem plausible to you?"

"Her climbing out the window? Not really," Helen admitted. "I'm just looking at all the angles."

"If she had been found in the bath, the suicide theory might hold water—excuse the pun. But turning up dead in the loch…That's definitely fishy."

"I suppose so. That means a murderer is at large, doesn't it? So, what's your best guess?"

"I'm nowhere ready to say."

"I knew a penny would be too little for your thoughts. What if I offered you a million pounds?"

"You don't have a million pounds. As far as I know."

Helen heaved a sigh as she walked in step beside him along the seemingly neverending wet road. "Unfortunately, no. School counsellors aren't *that* well paid. And no one in my family has died and left me anything." She was silent for a moment as the sign for Gleneagle Village came into view at the final bend in the road. "Does Moira have any family who would benefit from her death?"

"Only a father in Glasgow. But she had nothing, really, except her one-bedroom flat. If she left him anything, which I hope she didn't, he'd only drink it away. No, Moira was verra much alone in this world."

However, he refused to feel guilty. He had been good to her while they were together. He had not even complained when she suddenly decided it was her vocation to go and help the displaced in Baghdad. There she had fallen in love with an Australian photographer and written him a Dear John letter—when she eventually did decide to write. The contents of that letter made him flinch to this day. How she could have expected him to take her back when her lover returned to his wife in Sydney, he could not imagine.

"Here we are," he said unnecessarily when they reached the village with its stark gray stone cottages and tiny shops aligned on each side of the road.

Beside the Gleneagle Arms stood Murray's Newsagent's, the name stenciled in black letters across the orange awning. A small-paned window held so many For Sale notices and sundry announcements that it was almost impossible to see through to the inside. A bell rang as they entered. From the newspaper stand, a headline screamed, "Moor Murderer Strikes Again!" Rex picked up a newspaper for Alistair.

"Guid day tae ye, Mr. Graves," the wiry newsagent greeted from behind the counter, nodding a polite acknowledgment to Helen. "Whit can I dae for ye?"

"Is the pay phone down the street working?" Rex asked.

"Noo, but ye can use the phone in here—if ye'll mind the shop while I nip round the pub. Is it a local call?" Murray inquired with a suspicious glint in his eye.

"Aye."

The old man plunked the dial phone on Rex's side of the counter.

"I also need a tow truck," Rex informed him.

"Angus went fishin'. A'll send him tae the lodge when he returns."

Angus owned the local garage. Rex couldn't think of anyone else who could help with the tyres.

"A'll be reit back!" Murray gleefully raided the till, grabbed his cap, and disappeared through the door.

"He's a trusting soul," Helen remarked. "But then you *are* a Scottish barrister and an officer of the court."

"I suppose we could always run off with an armful of Mars Bars and Malteesers," Rex joked, gesturing toward the display of candy at the counter.

Pulling the old-fashioned black phone toward him, he dialed 9-9-9 and stated his emergency, adding detailed directions to the lodge. "Aye, that's right. Off the A82 ... between Invergarry and Laggan, north of the swing bridge. Aye, I'm sure the victim is dead," he told the dispatcher. "Murdered. When can the police get here? ... That long?"

"What's the delay?" Helen asked when he replaced the receiver.

"They're busy with the latest moor murder on top of all the emergencies caused by the rain. They'll be here as soon as they can, but since the victim is dead, the dispatcher said it wasn't a priority."

"But it's a murder!"

"I'm no sure she believed me, and all police resources are concentrated on hunting for Melissa Bates' killer. Every off-duty constable from Inverness to Perth and from the Atlantic to the North Sea has been deployed in the search."

"Isn't there a local bobby?"

"Not any more. But not much goes on in Gleaneagle except for the occasional drunken brawl."

"Until now."

"Until now." Rex dialed the lodge and then called the phone company to report that the line at his house was still down. "I wonder what's keeping Murray."

"Beer."

"I'll track him down next door and see if someone can take us back to the lodge."

"I'll go," Helen said. "He specifically asked you to mind the shop."

Rex did not much like the idea of Helen going into a pub by herself, but he knew she could take care of herself. After all, a group of lecherous old crofters and shopkeepers could not pose more of a threat than the hormonally active teenagers she worked with at her school.

While she was gone, he leaned against the counter and perused the story concerning the latest victim in the string of child murders on Rannoch Moor. The article did not offer many more details than Alistair had been able to provide. That the police had a traveling salesman from Inverness in custody was the latest development in the case. Chief Inspector Dalgerry from the Northern Constabulary was quoted as saying he was confident they had the right man for the murders and he hoped the public might rest more easy. A pair of photos accompanied the story, the pug-nosed Dalgerry contrasting starkly with the innocent young face of Melissa Bates.

The shop bell rang, and Helen re-entered with Murray and a midget of a man of about fifty with an impish countenance.

"This is Mr. Buccleugh, the fish monger," Helen announced. "He has kindly agreed to lend us his van—for ten pounds. I explained that our car broke down."

Good, Rex thought. He did not want to advertise a murder and have nosy-parkers turning up at the lodge and interfering with the evidence until after the police had left.

"I cleared oot the crates," Buccleugh said. "Ye can return the van on the morrow."

"Most obliged. Is there petrol in the tank?"

"Enough tae get ye tae Gleneagle Lodge an' back. Tis the yellow van parked ootside the pub." He gave Rex a key.

Rex paid the man and left money on the counter for the newspaper.

"Guid cheerio the nou!" Murray called after him as he and Helen left the shop.

Rex felt certain the locals exaggerated the Highland dialect for his benefit. But when he saw the van, he stopped short on the pavement. Now he knew he was the butt of a joke.

"No way!" This was what his Americanized son would say.

"It'll get us there," Helen said hesitantly.

The van was a mustard yellow Reliant Regal three-wheeler of the most basic design, with a bare metal floor and a window in the single door at the back. The interior reeked powerfully of haddock.

Installed on the upright seat, Rex manually rolled down his window to get rid of the stench and pressed the switch for the headlights. His knees embraced the wooden steering wheel in the cramped space, rendering it almost unnecessary to use his hands. Forcing the rickety gear shift in first, they wobbled off down the road. "This is right embarrassing," he muttered, imagining the villagers laughing their heads off behind their net curtains.

Helen opened the window on her side and stuck her face out for air. "What a ponk! But at least we don't have to walk."

"I'm verra grateful for the transportation, Helen, but was there really nothing else on offer?"

"We're lucky to get this. Seriously. They're a suspicious lot at the Gleneagle Arms. The looks I got! I suppose they don't get many visitors. They were still gossiping about a man who came in last night, who was 'not from around these parts.'" Helen mimicked the Highland accent, instilling the words with distrust and foreboding.

Rex's ears pricked right up. "What else did they say?"

"Well, I knew you'd be interested, so I asked the barman. He told me the man came in asking for directions to Gleneagle Lodge."

"Did you get a description?"

"Average height, around forty, and wearing something on his head. He seemed in a bad mood, apparently. Oh, and he was foreign."

"Around here that could mean he's from Inverness. Did the barman say what time the man came in?"

"About nine o'clock. And that's all he could tell me. Most of the regulars were in, he said, and he was busy serving, so he didn't pay much attention."

Rex concentrated on the slippery road as best he could while he assimilated this new piece of information.

Half a mile out of the village, the blare of a siren assailed them, followed by the persistent sound of a horn. Rex spotted the flashing ambulance in his rearview mirror and rolled onto the grass shoulder out of its way. The back end of the ambulance thundered into the distance.

"They'll get there before we do," Helen remarked.

"By a long chalk," Rex added, gunning the accelerator from a standstill as the single front wheel spun uselessly. "We are stuck in the mud."

ELEVEN

By the time Rex and Helen arrived back at Gleneagle Lodge in the three-wheeler, both of them mud-splattered from head to foot, the ambulance had left.

"It's all taken care of," Alistair said, coming out of the house to meet them. "The medics took the body to the morgue. Here's the number." He eyed the yellow van. "Um, may I ask … ?"

"It's all we had available to get us back here," Rex told him. "No one in the village wanted to venture out in this weather. The ambulance ran us off the road and we got stuck in the mud."

"I need to go and change," Helen said, starting toward the house.

"What about the police?" Rex asked Alistair.

"No show. And the ambulance had to dash off and respond to another call. I gave the medics all the information. They couldn't wait around for the police."

"So, what's new here? How are the guests bearing up?"

"The Allerdices are insisting they have to get back to their hotel. I persuaded them to wait until you returned. Shona is busy throwing together some lunch. Estelle and Flora are helping out."

"And the men?"

"Watching the soccer. All except Cuthbert, who stalked off somewhere in his hunting gear."

"Did he now?" Rex said tersely. "I asked him to keep an eye on things at the house."

"I couldn't stop him. He promised he wouldn't leave the property."

"Did he take his rifle?"

"Aye. He said to tell you not to worry as he didn't intend to kill anything."

This was not very reassuring. "What aboot you, Alistair? Are you okay?" His friend, hunched in his jacket against the wet weather, looked deathly pale. "You're soaked through."

"It was a wee bit emotional seeing that poor woman being carried off in a bag. I'm glad you were not here to witness it."

"Did the medics find anything unusual?"

"Nothing beyond the obvious. They were reluctant to move the body before the police arrived, but I told them we had fished it out of the loch hours ago and there was a chance it might start to decompose. It is, after all, summer. Not that you'd notice." Suddenly, Alistair grimaced. "Sorry. Didn't mean to sound callous. I forgot you two had been close."

"That's all right. It was awhile ago. And don't go believing everything Moira might have told you." Rex still couldn't altogether absorb the fact she was dead. "I'm just worried that removing the body prematurely might compromise eventual legal proceedings, in spite of the notes and photographs I took. Still, it's one less thing to worry about, I suppose. Now I can concentrate on the guests and try to find out who murdered her."

"I hope you're wrong about that. I still think it could have been an intruder. I mean, do you honestly think one of them could have done it?" Alistair thumbed toward the lodge.

"Killers come in all guises." Rex reached back into the van. "I brought you a paper. All available bobbies and brass are working on the Melissa Bates case. I was told the police would respond to our emergency when they could."

"I have no doubt you'll figure it out by yourself." Alistair gave him a reassuring pat on the shoulder and directed him under the porch.

"I don't have much to go on. Most of the evidence will have been washed away in the rain. I don't suppose anyone came to fix the phone in my absence so I can call the coroner?"

"No visitors except for the medics."

"There's not one mobile to be had in the village. Helen inquired at the pub. Too much to hope that Shona found hers … ?"

"She searched everywhere."

Rex sighed in despair. "I arranged for the local mechanic to come. Until then," he said, pointing to the Reliant, "this is our only set of wheels."

"I wouldn't be seen dead in it," Alistair declared. "The good news is I doubt anybody will bother sabotaging it."

"I should lock it in the stable, just in case—though I doubt it would make it up the hill in the mud. It barely managed the other side on a proper road. Perhaps I should have left it at the top of the hill, but I thought I should keep an eye on it since it's on loan."

"Are you going to keep everyone here?" Alistair asked.

"At least until I've spoken to the coroner. Perhaps he can shed some light on events."

"It's a she. Dr. Sheila Macleod. I impressed upon the medic how urgent this was. In fact, I even got his number." The look of complicit satisfaction on Alistair's face left Rex in no doubt as to his meaning.

"What happened to your solicitor friend? The one who arranged the sale of this house? I'm assuming you and he ... "

"We had a tiff. I left Edinburgh without my phone on purpose. I hoped—childishly—that he would call and wonder where I was, and I didn't want to be constantly checking my messages in the hope that he had."

"I see."

"Sorry about that. However, to redeem myself, I begged a favour off the young medic—John. His aunt just so happens to be Dr. Macleod. He'll tell her to get right on it, and she'll contact the procurator fiscal if she determines the death suspicious."

"I'm glad something is working to our advantage at last." Rex glanced at the house. "I'll join you inside in just a minute. I want to take a quick look around first."

He found the pony grazing among his dripping flowerbeds, in the spot where he had left the ladder. Donnie must have let her out of the stable. He could at least have put her in the meadow, Rex fumed to himself.

"Off with you! Shoo!" he exclaimed, waving his arms at the Shetland, without venturing too close in case she decided to take a bite out of him with her big ivory teeth—the size of piano keys.

Strolling off, she started nonchalantly nibbling on a rhododendron bush. Rex, though incensed, attended to the more urgent matter of examining the ground beneath the bathroom window. Horse hooves had churned up the soil and grass around the feet of the ladder. No other prints had survived the downpour. However, a thorny vine growing up the wall had been flattened where it grew out of the soil. Moira's body must have landed there. Unless that, too, was the horse's doing. Rex regretted not having taken a look before he left for the village, but he had expected the police to arrive.

He followed the most direct route across the lawn to the jetty where the boat was moored. Rid of its tarpaulin, the bottom had filled with rainwater. Rex looked back toward the house. A distance of not more than thirty feet, but no one looking from a window would have seen anything through the deluge the previous night.

All the perpetrator had to do was transport the body to the loch, dump it in the boat, and row out as far as possible before dispatching it into the chilly depths. In the low visibility, that person may not have noticed the islet where the corpse was ultimately washed up among the reeds.

Mulling over his meager findings, Rex entered the house and added his boots to those in the hallway. He compared the samples of soil and plant debris from the flowerbed on his to the mud on the guests' footwear, and found something of botanical interest. Subdued male voices emanated from the library. Upon walking into the room, he saw that the television was switched on to the news. The newspaper photograph of seven-year-old Melissa Bates filled the screen, her dark hair braided on either side of a heart-shaped face.

Alistair, standing in the middle of the room, muted the sound when he saw Rex. "Nothing new," he reported.

"It's si—sick," Donnie stuttered from the sofa where he sat beside his dad. "Who'd want to hurt a wee girl?"

"I hope they got the sadistic bastard this time," Hamish replied.

Rex noticed that the men had all helped themselves to his stock of Guinness. Cans littered the end tables. Rob Roy sat in his leather wing armchair, a beer clasped in his lap.

"I pray this time they did," Alistair concurred. "I hope they checked out Collins' alibi thoroughly first. It's funny how he always seems to have a good one available."

"If it's not Collins after all, you can't go on blaming yourself for his acquittal," Rex pointed out.

"I know when someone is lying. He'd have to prove he was more than a hundred miles from Rannoch Moor yesterday before I'd believe him, and it would have to be God vouching for him."

"Rannoch Moor is a vast stretch of wasteland," Hamish said, slurring his speech and causing Rex to wonder exactly how many beers he had consumed. "I visited there once and remember thinking I'd never want to break down in a lonely pla*sh* like that. They cut down most of the trees, you know, to prevent villains from lurking in the fore*sh*. Have you ever been there, Rob?"

"Can't say that I have."

"I know it quite well," Rex told them. "I used to hike across Rannoch Moor, precisely because of the solitude. There's a lot of wildlife, as you'd expect in such an unpopulated area."

Rex actually knew the area better than most. Surrounded by mountains, Rannoch Moor brooded across fifty square miles, rising to over one thousand feet above sea level, the whole substratum of granite gouged by glens, slashed by rivers, and pitted with lochs. Gnarled roots of old pine trees from the ancient Caledonian forest beckoned from the peat. No road connected the moor from east to west, where deep bog swallowed everything put in its path.

By virtue of being so desolate, it provided a haven for all sorts of bird, animal, and plant life, which he had duly noted on his hikes. The shores and islets of trout-filled lochs attracted goosander, black-throated diver, and red-breasted merganser, while curlew and grouse haunted the heathery slopes. Golden eagles and osprey circled the rocky summits where hare and roe deer roamed undisturbed for the most part. Fragrant myrtle abounded in the bogs and a particular plant grew exclusively in the region, which was indeed a treasure trove for the observant nature lover.

"No sign of Cuthbert?" he asked in a casual tone.

"He went off in his daft hat after the ambulan*sh* left," Hamish told him. "He said your advocate friend Alistair could take over."

"Trust that aristocratic twit to shirk his duties," Alistair remarked.

Rex could not agree more. The investigation of Moira's death was not proceeding as anticipated, but he was on one right track. He could feel it in the tingle at the back of his neck—a sure sign he was onto something important.

TWELVE

REX LEFT THE MEN to discuss the Moor murders and went to check on the women, who were bustling around in the kitchen, chatting nonstop as women do. However, the chatter ceased when he entered. Presumably they had been talking about Moira.

"Oh, hello, Rex," Shona said in a fluster, drying a wine glass. "We're reheating the venison stew for lunch. There are loads of leftovers from last night, so we won't starve."

"Did you pick up any groceries in the village?" Estelle Farquharson wanted to know. "We're about to run out of milk."

"It skipped my mind." Rex glanced for assistance at Helen, who was preparing a green salad.

"I told you, Estelle," she explained. "We went to find a phone and to get hold of the garage owner. Unfortunately, the villagers don't seem to feel a pressing need to get anything done in a hurry. I suppose it would all be rather quaint if we weren't in such a fix."

"Well, when *is* the man with the tow truck due to arrive?" Estelle demanded.

"Soon," Helen replied firmly.

Rex privately thought they might not see him until next week. Equipped with plaid pot holders, Estelle removed the casserole of stew from the Aga and proceeded out the door. "I'm setting up the food in the dining room, buffet-style like breakfast," she called over her shoulder.

"She has completely taken over," Helen remarked, following her out of the kitchen with the bowl of salad.

Flora brought up the rear with a basket of bread rolls.

"Any luck with your phone, Shona?" Rex asked.

Mrs. Allerdice shrugged helplessly. "I must have left it somewhere I can't hear it. I've looked and looked. Well, I suppose it will turn up."

Yes, but *where?* Rex asked himself. "Shona," he began. "When I saw you standing by the front door last night as I was going down to the library with Alistair, you ... well, you looked a wee bit suspicious."

She dropped her eyes to the floor.

"Care to tell me what you were doing?"

"You won't tell Hamish?"

"Tell him what?"

"I went outside for a puff."

"What?"

"He doesn't know I smoke. I have to sneak around and hide my cigarettes. I have breath mints so he won't notice. It's my one weakness."

"Perhaps your husband could help you quit, if you'd just confess—"

"Not Hamish! He'd kill me. He'd say we cannot afford it, and he's quite right." Mrs. Allerdice wrung the dishtowel in her hands. "In fact, I'm getting a craving now."

"Listen, Shona. The important thing right this minute is to remember what time it was when you went out for your smoke last night."

"Oh, that's easy. It was ten minutes past twelve. I looked at my watch. I time my smokes so Hamish doesn't get suspicious. I told him I had to go to the loo."

"How long where you outside?"

"Five minutes. I'd just stepped back inside when I saw you coming down the stairs with Alistair. A second before, I'd heard a very loud thud, like Rob Roy described, only I didn't mention it earlier because I didn't want Hamish to find out what I'd been up to. In fact, I thought at the time it might be him coming to catch me oot."

"The time is very important," Rex told her. "If you're sure it was a quarter past twelve when you heard the sound …"

"I'm positive."

Rex mentally drew up a timeline. Moira's body had in all probability been dropped from the window at the time Shona stated. He had been in bed for a short while before Alistair came to find him to tell him the news of the latest moor victim. That would explain why Alistair had not heard the sound himself, which he would have done had he stayed in the library. "What you've just told me is vital information," he told Shona frostily. "Now we can pinpoint more accurately the moment of Moira's death."

"Aye, I see. I'm so sorry." Tears sprung to her eyes.

"There, there." Rex handed her a paper towel. "I'm glad you came forward."

Shona nodded, sniveling. "You won't tell Hamish?"

"Not unless I absolutely have to." Far be it for him to interfere in marital affairs. "What was your husband doing when you left him to come downstairs?"

"Taking a look at the radiator to see if he could fix the leak."

"Did he?" Rex asked hopefully.

"No."

"Ah, well. One other thing... Did you two have an argument this morning?"

"Aye, we did. But it's personal." Mrs. Allerdice pursed her lips together defiantly. This must be a bigger deal than the smoking, Rex deduced.

"I won't pry further for now," he told her. He would see if he could get more out of Hamish. "And thank you for helping with lunch."

While the guests were busy flocking around the dining table, Rex began a systematic search of the house for Shona's phone, starting in the hall and looking in all the obvious places, including inside the umbrella stand, and proceeding to the nooks and crannies in the cupboard beneath the stairs. Fortunately, he'd not had the house a long time, and so only a minimal amount of clutter had been given the chance to accumulate in the storage spaces.

Next he rummaged through the library, poking around in the open log fireplace, which had not been lit. Useful evidence had been found in a fireplace before in one of his cases.

Not this time. He straightened up and thought hard for a moment, wondering where someone might hide a compact device—

or two, for it was quite possible that if Moira had brought a cell phone with her to Gleneagle, it had been stolen as well. His eyes lingered, unfocused in thought, on the piled logs. The fireplaces in the upstairs bedrooms had been boarded up and wallpapered over, until he'd had the McCallum brothers restore the original Victorian grates. Prior to central heating, coal had been used to warm the rooms. The coal shed! Now that would be a handy place to ditch a phone.

Just off the kitchen extended a small patio for the trash bins. He accessed the shed by walking under the eaves. Unlikely Shona would look here, he thought, opening the shed door. And why should she? She thought she had misplaced her phone, never imagining someone had snatched it. The interior of the shed was dark. Very little coal was stored here, since it only served to fuel the seldom-used heater in the stable. The reconditioned Aga stove in the kitchen ran on gas.

After hurrying back inside to fetch a flashlight from the kitchen drawer, he returned to the shed and directed the beam into the sooty corners, without finding what he was looking for. Just to be sure, he grabbed a shovel and turned over the small pile of coals, and almost missed them: two almost identical black cell phones, blackened further with coal dust. Not seeing any fingerprints, he wiped the coal dust off with a rag and slipped Moira's into his pocket. The other he hid upstairs in the airing closet under a pile of towels.

"Rex, what on earth are you doing sneaking about?" Estelle demanded from the stairs.

"Sneaking?" he inquired. She made him sound like Shona Allerdice.

"I saw you go out through the kitchen door and then scurry upstairs in a most furtive manner. What are you up to?"

Rex felt like telling her to mind her own business. It was his house, after all. Instead, he reminded himself she had a right to ask. A murder had been committed under his roof and she was no doubt suspicious, and probably not just a little bit scared.

"Actually, I wanted to ask you if Cuthbert was back from his walk yet? He's been gone awhile."

"The silly man has probably gone and got himself lost. Now then, Rex. I know when I'm being fobbed off. What is all the secrecy about?"

Damn the woman! He hummed and hawed. "If I tell you, it means taking you into my confidence."

"Brownie's honour and all that."

Rex thought quickly. "Well, I bought a gift as a surprise for Helen and hid it in the coal shed. But I was worried it might get damp with all the rain, so I moved it upstairs."

Estelle looked charmed. "Well, whatever is it?"

"I don't know if I should divulge …"

"Mum's the word."

"It's a sheep." It was all he could think of as he looked at the woman.

"What?"

"A toy sheep. Actually, it's a lamb. Helen's very partial to them. Lambs hold a special meaning for us. Our love blossomed in the spring, so it's sort of symbolic." Rex stared with embarrassment at his feet. Was that really the best he could do?

"Rex, how terribly sweet!" Estelle bleated. "I never suspected you had a sentimental side to you!" She planted an enthusiastic kiss on his cheek. "I'm sure Helen will be thrilled!"

"You won't tell?"

"Cross my heart, hope to die. When are you going to give it to her?"

"Estelle! Where the hell is that woman?" Hamish's voice boomed rudely from downstairs.

"Oh, drat," she whispered to Rex. "I said I would help the Allerdice women do the dishes. Hamish is such a tyrant. But I suppose Flora and Shona *have* been bearing the brunt of the work with Helen." In a loud voice, she added, "Well, you're quite right, Rex. It *is* dismal weather we're having."

With a conspiratorial wink, she galumphed back down the carpeted steps, her shadow magnified against the wall by the lamp hanging from the ceiling in the windowless stairwell. The closer the object to the light source, the larger the shadow, Rex remembered from a school project. If Estelle had been wearing her curlers last night, it would fit Flora's description of the grotesque apparition.

Mrs. Farquharson had not batted an eyelid when he mentioned the coal shed. Was she innocent or else adept at concealing her guilt? In any case, Rex realized he would have to be more careful as he pursued his investigation. "'Softly, softly catchee monkey,'" he chanted under his breath.

Or was it a question of catching the sheep?

THIRTEEN

"A SHEEP?" HELEN ASKED incredulously, cornering Rex in the dining room after his quick lunch. "You mean a cuddly toy? Urgh. Tell me you didn't."

"To help you count sheep so you fall asleep quicker."

"I'll think of Estelle and get nightmares. What are you up to, Rex?" She cocked her head at him with a look of amused curiosity.

"I canna tell you just yet. Though it is interesting to note that Estelle is incapable of holding a secret for long."

"She confided in Shona, who came to whisper the surprise to me and tell me not to say anything to you."

"Women!" Rex rolled his eyes, at a complete loss as to what went on in their brains sometimes.

"Well, as soon as I heard the cuddly lamb part, I knew something was amiss, so I just tried to act delighted, as was expected of me. Couldn't you have given me a diamond or something?"

"A diamond?" he repeated. Did she mean a ring? An engagement ring?

Helen shrugged in despair. "Oh, just *anything*, I suppose—but not a cutesy toy!"

"It's verra realistic looking. Woolly grey hair, wee brown eyes, a long snout." He was describing Estelle down to a tee, and Helen chuckled.

"You are so wicked, Rex! Oh, well, I know better than to waste my time trying to pry your little scheme out of you, but I'm glad you're onto something."

"Well, mebbe." Rex fingered his ginger whiskers. He had not taken the time to shave or shower that morning and did not have time now. "I should talk to the guests in turn." He glanced at the cleared table. "Here would be fine."

"Shall I leave the water jug and glasses?"

"Aye. I'll start with the Allerdices since they're in the greatest hurry to leave."

"I'll send Hamish in while Shona helps me in the kitchen."

"Good idea. I want to ask him who took a peek at Moira's body while she lay dead in the stable." And why he had found coal dust on Hamish's shoes when he went back to examine the boots in the hall.

"He's such a creep," Helen remarked with a shudder.

A few minutes later, Hamish entered the dining room and shut the door behind him.

"Come and sit down, Hamish," Rex said from the oak table. "I just want to ask everybody a few questions before they leave."

"Why are you starting with me?" Allerdice asked in a belligerent tone, the spidery veins lacing his bulbous nose reddening sharply.

"Because I'm sure you need to get back to the hotel. The Farquharsons and Mr. Frazer planned to stay until tomorrow anyway."

Hamish visibly relaxed. "Well, you can talk to Shona and Flora next. The lad went off somewhere with the pony."

"This is right awkward," Rex began, splaying his hands on the table. "But I cannot help but notice that Donnie is a bit slow."

"Aye, in some ways. But once you show him how to do something, he's reliable and willing. And he has a special touch with animals, always brings stray cats and dogs home. He's kind-hearted that way."

"I can see that. And what aboot wi' girls? How does he get on wi' women?"

"You mean a girlfriend? He's never had one, but he's only seventeen."

"The reason I ask is that Moira's body was tampered with while she was in Donnie's care in the stable."

Hamish's already florid face grew an even ruddier shade, infusing with blood all the way to his receding hairline. "Och, he might have taken a quick look, but I'm sure he didna mean her any disrespect."

"You were there too, helping him in the stable."

"It must've happened while my back was turned."

Rex wondered. The man would not meet his gaze. "Going back to last night ... You spent a bit of time talking to Moira."

"She spoke to everybody. Such a nice lass. Verra outgoing. What a shame ..."

"Did you see her after she went upstairs?"

"No, I never saw her again until she turned up in the loch."

Rex shook his head slowly at him. "Now, I know that's not true. I heard you approach her when she was aboot to take a bath."

Hamish's countenance darkened. "So?"

"She sounded a wee bit upset."

"She was leading me on earlier. I dinna know why she would suddenly get so agitated."

"There are boundaries, Hamish. Approaching a woman in her dressing gown might leave her feeling a bit vulnerable."

"Look, I dinna know what happened to your ex-girlfriend. She slammed the door in my face. I was worried she would make a scene, so I just left."

"You did *not* sound too happy aboot it."

"Do you like rejection?" Hamish asked with a scowl.

"I tend to avoid getting into situations where I might get rejected."

Hamish's body seemed to implode as he sank back in the chair. "Aye, well. 'Nothing ventured, nothing gained,' as they say."

"I need to ask you aboot an argument you had with your wife this morning."

"She told you?" Hamish expostulated.

"Helen heard you."

"Is this placed bugged? There's no bloody privacy!" Hamish paused a beat before resuming. "It was aboot something that happened a long time ago. It's not relevant to your ex-girlfriend's murder."

"I need all the facts, if only to be able to eliminate them. Do you have any secrets you keep from your wife?"

"Shona?"

"Is there another wife?"

Hamish glared at him. "Of course not! I only meant, why should I keep any secrets from her?"

"She may keep some from you."

"Like the smoking, you mean?"

"You know?"

"Aye."

"Wouldn't it be simpler if you just told her you knew?"

"If she thought I condoned her habit, she'd just smoke more, and we canna afford it."

Rex wondered what bad habit of his own Hamish indulged in to make him tolerate his wife's aberration.

"Look," the hotelier said with a sigh. "My wife's right upset aboot Moira. We had a drowning in our loch a couple of summers ago, if you must know. A wee lass at the hotel."

Rex glanced up from his spiral notebook and studied the heavy face in front of him. "I'm sorry."

"I didna want to bring it up as it's not the sort of thing you want to broadcast. The parents were in the sauna at the time. You know how bairns are. She wandered away from the person supposed to be minding her and waded into the loch. She'd been talking aboot the magic dragon. She was right fascinated wi' the idea of a fantastical monster living in the water."

"How old was she?"

"Six or seven." Hamish wrung his hands. "It was an accident, but all the same … Terrible publicity at the time. It's a godsend there's renewed interest in the Loch Lochy Monster. Rob Roy has promised not to allude to the drowning."

"This was the subject of the argument between you and your wife?"

"Aye. Well, it's a long story." Hamish scratched his sandpaper stubble. "Will that be all?"

"Just one other thing. Did you need to get more coal for the heater in the stable?"

"What do you mean?"

"I just wondered if Donnie was warm enough last night."

"Och, he was snug as a bug in a rug. Plenty warm enough."

Interesting that Hamish had not taken the bait, Rex noted in his pad. "Thank you. I'll talk to Shona now."

Hamish rose abruptly from the dining table. "Please treat her with kid gloves. She had a nervous breakdown two years ago. I'm worried this might set her off again."

Rex sat back in the uncomfortable Queen Anne style chair, which the interior designer had recommended and which he had been gullible enough to buy. He should, in retrospect, have let Helen choose the furnishings, but he had been afraid of being dragged around furniture shops and asked for opinions that would never be listened to anyway. So much easier to present her with the finished product so they could get on with the business of enjoying the house.

Obviously, that was not going to be this weekend.

FOURTEEN

"You wanted to see me?" Shona asked timidly from the door-way.

"Make yourself comfortable," Rex said bouncing up from the table and pulling out a chair for her. "Would you like some water?"

"Och, no, I'm fine."

"I'm sorry to bring up something upsetting that happened two years ago, but Hamish said you were troubled by the situation with Moira in view of that event…"

Crossing her arms, Shona rubbed the sleeves of her homespun sweater as though she might be cold. Finally she nodded and began to speak. "When your friend was found in the loch this morning, it all came flooding back. That wee lass that drowned in our loch was brought out of the water in her father's arms. He dove in after her but it was too late." Mrs. Allerdice dried away a tear with her woolen cuff. "He blamed us, but it wasna Flora's fault. She was only nineteen at the time and was doing them a favour, looking after their bairn while they were gallivanting in the sauna."

"What happened exactly?"

"The wee lass was building a sand castle on the strip of shore-line, which we call the beach. Flora was sunbathing and reading a magazine. One of our other guests, a young American, went over to talk to her and, well, that's when Amy took off. Her father spotted her from his bedroom window and tried to attract Flora's attention. He rushed down to the loch and swam out to the spot where he had last seen the child."

"What a tragedy." Rex comfortingly squeezed Shona's wrist across the table.

"Flora was devastated. There had been a budding relationship between her and the American—Brad, a young architect from Boston. But it was never the same after that. Things became strained and, in any case, he had to fly home the following week. He never contacted her. Flora was verra disappointed."

"Were there other guests staying at the hotel?"

"Aye, we had a full house that June. None of them ever came back. It was the parents' fault for not taking care of the bairn themselves," Shona declared bitterly. "It wasna Flora's job."

"So you are hoping to deflect interest away from that incident by promoting the Lizzie of Loch Lochy story." Rex almost said "hoax" but stopped himself just in time. "And Rob Roy is proving instrumental in this project."

"Well, aye," Shona said, brightening up. "He's verra serious about this article he's writing. Yesterday he went to take photographs from the far side of the loch, aboot ten miles to the south, where old Cameron saw Lizzie."

"Did he walk?"

"Aye, he came up from Glasgow by train. I packed him some egg sandwiches, crisps, and an orange, since he said he would not be back for lunch. He saw some ripples in the water, but wasna able to get a picture."

Rex shook his head in sympathy. "It's a right elusive creature, isn't it?" Then, "It looks like Rob Roy might be playing court to Flora," he added tentatively.

"Och, no. At any rate, I don't think Flora is interested."

"You don't approve of Rob Roy?"

"Well," Shona replied in a lowered voice. "I dinna think he has much money. He's a nice young man, but Flora could do better. In fact, since you bring it up, that's what Hamish and I were in disagreement aboot this morning. He thinks I have unrealistic expectations regarding Flora's future. He said the romance between our daughter and the architect from Boston was all in my head—and hers. He spoke to Brad regarding his intentions, he said, and the lad acted cool and surprised. But men often don't have a clue aboot these things."

"Quite," Rex said in a noncommittal tone. "Going back to Moira's death—and I regret making you dwell on it—did you notice anything unusual last night, either in the way people were behaving or perhaps later, when everybody had gone to bed? You might have remembered something..."

Shona sighed and looked around the room for inspiration. Apparently she found none, for she drew her thin lips together until they were mere lines in her face and shook her head resolutely. "I wish I could help. I mean, other than your friend flirting with all the men..."

"You mean Moira?"

"Oh, aye, not Helen. She would never do that to you. She loves and respects you. That's obvious."

Rex pondered this. Did that mean Shona did not think Moira had loved and respected him? Since they were no longer together, it did not much matter whether she had or not—though had she not still loved him, would she have chased after him to Florida and then to the Highlands?

Gazing upon Shona's downcast face, it suddenly dawned on him. She was drawing a comparison between Hamish and Moira. She was suggesting that her husband could not love or respect her or else he wouldn't make a pass at every attractive woman within grasp. But, according to Helen, Moira had been trying to make him jealous.

"All right, hen," he said kindly. "I'll just have a word with Flora, and Donnie when he returns, and then you can get back to the hotel as soon as we get your van fixed." Presumably the police would arrive before then.

"What aboot Rob Roy?"

"You can wait for him or else he can walk back after I've spoken to him. He has his walking boots and it's only four miles as the crow flies."

Shona slipped out of her chair and called to Flora. The girl sidled into the room and her mother closed the door softly between them.

"I want to be here when you question Donnie," Flora told Rex. "He'll only clam up if I'm not."

"Where is he?"

"He'll be around somewhere. He prefers the outdoors to being cooped up in a house."

"Of course you can sit in when I talk to him. I can see how close the two of you are."

Appeased, Flora took a chair. "My dad said the two of you discussed the drowning back at the hotel two summers ago."

"He wanted me to be aware of the situation before I talked to your mother, so as not to upset her."

"It was awful," Flora said. "It affected everyone."

"Who else was on the beach at the time?"

"I was there with Brad." Flora swallowed with difficulty. "I was distracted."

Rex poured her a glass of water. She was rather a plain lass, he decided, but with a bit of effort, she could have been attractive. Her features were pleasant enough and her dreamy eyes, pale and gray as mist, lent her face a certain wistfulness.

"I was supposed to keep an eye on Amy for part of the morning," she explained. "My mother begged me to. I'd planned to spend time with Brad since he was leaving to go back to the States the following week. He'd talked about visiting Urquhart Castle on the shores of Loch Ness and asked if I would come along as a tour guide."

Rex didn't think "tour guide" sounded very romantic on the part of a suitor, but tried to keep his expression neutral.

"My mother said it was good for business if I did a spot of free babysitting. She said I could visit the castle with Brad another time and not to seem so eager. When he came up to me and started talking, I forgot all about Amy."

"Were you and Brad the only two adults on the beach?"

"It's not really a beach, just a slip of sand along the loch. There was a couple from the hotel, but they were facing the hotel. They didn't see anything."

"What about Donnie?"

"He was roe deer stalking that day. He started as a ghillie when he was fourteen. Why is the drowning at our hotel relevant to Moira's murder?"

"The drowning at Loch Lochy may not be relevant at all. What happened afterwards?"

Flora folded her arms into her chest. "It was ruled an accident. Eventually the press went away. Brad never wrote or called. I was heartbroken about the whole thing. I think he blamed me for Amy's death. He didna know she was supposed to be in my care. I could actually blame *him*. If he hadna stopped on the beach, I would have been paying attention to her."

"Do you plan to stay on at your parents' hotel?"

"I wish I could leave. I was about to go off to university when the accident happened. But I was too depressed afterwards. I decided to wait a year. And, well, I'm still here—as you can see."

"I don't suppose you can tell me more aboot the shadow you saw on the stairs last night?"

Flora shifted in her chair. "I've already told you."

"Was the person going up or down the stairs?"

"Down—no, up. I told you, I canna remember."

"Can you recall what sort of knife? Was it a kitchen knife or perhaps a hunting knife like Donnie keeps in a sheath on his belt—?"

"No! And now that I think aboot it, I dinna think it can have been a knife. It wasna sharp, but it was long."

"A hunting rifle?"

Flora gazed right into his eyes. "I think so. And just so you know, Donnie doesn't have a rifle. Dad won't let him keep one."

"There's only one person here who owns a gun, as far as I know," Rex told her, wondering what was keeping Cuthbert. He needed to ask Mr. Farquharson how long he had been talking to Moira at the bathroom door and what had been said. Helen had crept up on him as he was listening at the foot of the stairs and he hadn't heard the rest of the conversation.

"One more question," he told Flora. "Are you sure it was half past twelve when you saw this person?"

"Aye, I believe so. Can I go now?"

Rex nodded and thanked her. "Could you ask Mrs. Farquharson to step in?"

Rex made a note in his pad and underlined it. He was sure the girl was lying.

FIFTEEN

ESTELLE POPPED IN AS soon as Flora opened the door. "I was waiting in line," she told Rex, striding into the dining room. "Is this the hot seat?" she asked, pulling out the chair Flora had vacated.

"Sit anywhere you like."

Estelle plunked herself down on the Queen Anne chair and propped her arms on the table, regarding him expectantly. "Shoot."

"Well, ehm, let me see." Rex perused the notes in his pad. "I can't recall if you said you had reason to go downstairs after you went to bed last night."

"I think I may. I usually have to get up at least once in the night, especially if I've had a lot of alcohol to drink. I have what is commonly known as an overactive bladder."

"I had that problem myself awhile back. It turned out to be an enlarged prostate. So, you think you may have gone downstairs at some point."

"Yes, pretty certain I did, actually."

"But you have no idea when?"

122

"Afraid not."

"Presumably you tried the upstairs bathroom first?"

Estelle nodded. "Must have found it occupied."

"Were you wearing your dressing gown?"

"I'm sure I was, dear man! Though I did have my nightie on underneath."

"Were you carrying anything?"

Estelle leaned forward across the table. "What on earth are you suggesting? That I was the shadow Flora saw on the stairs?"

"It fits your description, if you were wearing your curlers. She thought you might have been holding a rifle."

"Didn't she say a knife? And, anyway, wasn't the rifle in the room with the leaky radiator? Cuthbert said you retrieved it from the cupboard this morning."

"That's where I put it yesterday afternoon, out of harm's way."

"You didn't hide it very well. Usually Bertie can't find anything."

"It wasn't my intention to hide it, exactly. I just did not want your husband using it on my land. I happen to believe in the sacredness of life."

"Nonsense," Estelle said affably. "I'm sure you eat beef and pork and all the rest of it. Don't think for a minute they're slaughtered in a more humane way."

"In any case," Rex resumed. "That room wasn't supposed to be used. Then Moira turned up and everybody ended up staying because of the rainstorm, and I had to put Mr. and Mrs. Allerdice in there."

"Well, perhaps it was one of them on the stairs with the gun, though I have to say I can't picture Shona with a rifle. Such a tame little thing. More likely her brute of a husband."

"Flora said something about Gorgon-like hair. Hamish is slightly lacking in that department."

"Perhaps he had something over his head to keep off the rain."

This was something Rex had not considered.

"Are you going to be questioning your friend Alistair?" she asked.

"I already spoke to him at length before lunch. Why?"

"Well, there's something a bit secretive about him. Now, I know he's a colleague of yours, but he seems rather mopey and brooding, in a Heathcliff sort of way, if you follow my drift. Devilishly handsome, of course. No wonder the women swoon over him. I just think there might be something going on there."

Not what you might think, Rex said to himself, unwilling to out Alistair. Changing tack, he asked, "I saw that there was coal dust on your shoes, and I'm curious as to how it got there."

"You know very well," Mrs. Farquharson reprimanded. "I went to the coal shed to see what you were doing. I must have stood in some."

"I might simply have been fetching coal," Rex told her.

"But you didn't come back with any, so I followed you up the stairs."

"And you gave away my secret about Helen's surprise."

"Oh, dear. Did that feckless Allerdice woman spill the beans?"

"She *is* one to gossip, Estelle. I cannot imagine why you told her."

"*Mea culpa.* She gave me her word she wouldn't say anything."

124

"Her word did not prove to be of much value," Rex said pointedly. Estelle's neither.

"Oh, did she tell Helen?"

"Aye." Rex glared at her from beneath profuse ginger eyebrows, a look he used to good effect in court when confronted by a recalcitrant witness.

"My dear man, I feel horrible. Shona somehow managed to wheedle it out of me. She thought we were discussing Alistair."

"Why would she think that?"

"Because he's a friend of yours and he *has* been acting a bit strangely. He seemed fine last night and then today he's been morose and hasn't spoken two words to Flora."

"He has a lot on his mind. Why is Shona so interested in Alistair?"

Estelle stared at him, dumbstruck. "Well, it's obvious. She has designs on him for her daughter. If she could marry Flora off to a wealthy man, the hotel would be secure. It's in trouble." She leaned farther across the table. "Who else's shoes did you find coal dust on? I didn't buy for one minute that you had hidden a woolly lamb in the coal shed. You have more sense. So, tell me. What were you really doing out there?"

Rex smiled wolfishly at her. "Now, Estelle, you don't really expect me to divulge any more sensitive information to you, do you?"

Estelle straightened in her chair and sighed in defeat. "I suppose not. I've been a complete idiot, suspecting you in the first place and then blabbing to Shona."

"No real harm done," Rex conceded. "But now Helen will expect a diamond ring." He put a finger to his lips.

Mrs. Farquharson gasped. "A ring?"

He shot her a warning look.

She nodded solemnly. "Cross my heart twice and hope to die if I tell this time."

You didn't die last time you made that promise and broke it, Rex thought. "Who's still in the house?" he asked.

"That journalist. Bertie and the Allerdice boy are outside somewhere."

"I'll speak to Rob Roy next." Rex thanked Mrs. Farquharson and waited for his next interviewee. He hoped Donnie would return soon, since he could not reasonably detain the Allerdices any longer. On the other hand, there was no sign of the tow truck and, short of taking the three-wheeler, which could not possibly transport the whole family and their guest up the hill, there was no way out. Only Rob Roy and Donnie had worn footwear suitable for a long walk back to the hotel across muddy hills and water-logged glens.

Beardsley's owlish face peered through the opening in the door. "Heard you wanted a chat."

Rex gestured toward the chair. "Just an informal Q & A so I can help get the police up to speed when they arrive. They're tied up with the latest child abduction on Rannoch Moor for now."

"Aye, it's still monopolizing the news."

"Not the sort of story you'd want to cover, I suppose?"

"Och, I prefer to stick to nature subjects. The editor at the *Inverness News-Press* is really interested in my article on Lizzie. It's a huge regional paper and would be a stepping stone to the nationals. I just need one or two good photographs."

"Shona said you had a sighting yesterday."

"Aye, I saw Lizzie all right, but she wouldna surface. These creatures have a sixth sense. That's why it's usually fishermen who catch a glimpse of them. They'll be sitting quietly in their boats with their lines baited when suddenly the sea monster appears out of the blue. If I could prove the existence of Cousin Bessie in Loch Lown, it would make headline news."

"I assure you, nothing like that exists here."

"But you said you hadn't plumbed the depths. Some of the lochs are hundreds and hundreds of feet deep."

"If I do spot her, Rob Roy, I'll let you know. In the meantime, this is private property and I don't want any nosy thrill-seekers trespassing on my land."

"Understood."

"Of course, Loch Lochy is a different matter. Mr. and Mrs. Allerdice would welcome the publicity. How long do you intend on staying there?"

"I'm not sure exactly, but I'm that close to getting a photo." The journalist indicated about an inch between his thumb and forefinger. "Just one good shot and I'll have it wrapped up."

"Have you ever visited Loch Lochy before?" Rex asked.

"Never. My interest in plesiosaurs is fairly recent. Too much has been done on the Loch Ness Monster."

"Aye, it's been going on a long time. I'm surprised Nessie is still alive."

"They live as long as elephants."

"Is that so?" Rex scooted his chair back from the table and crossed his legs. "Might there be another reason you wish to prolong your stay at the hotel?"

Rob Roy regarded him darkly behind his clear lenses.

"Flora?" Rex suggested with an innocent smile. "Are ye not just a wee bit sweet on the lass?"

The journalist relaxed in his chair. "Oh, I see. I thought maybe you were under the impression I was freeloading off the Allerdices and, well, I resented the, ah, implication."

"Och, noo," Rex emphatically replied. "They are indebted to your interest in their loch."

Beardsley smiled tightly. Rex could tell the journalist was not sure if he was being sarcastic or not. He couldn't see what was going on with Beardsley's hands behind the table, but guessed the fingers were wriggling with impatience.

"And it is such a pretty spot. Where did you say you were from again?"

"Brora, originally."

"That's north of Inverness, isn't it?"

"Look," Rob Roy cut in. "I promised Flora I'd go after Donnie. He's always wandering off somewhere and causing her to fret."

"Aye, of course. Thank you for your time. I'd like to speak to the lad as well."

After the journalist left, Rex went to find Helen and located her upstairs putting clean towels in the guest bathroom.

"I suppose we might as well use this bathroom," she said.

"Might as well," Rex agreed. "I should have left it in the state I found it so the police could take a look, but I didn't know then that Moira was missing, and the water was seeping through to the library ceiling." That would have been around the time Moira drowned in the bath. "So much for preservation of the scene and non-contamination of evidence," he added ruefully.

"It's not as if you found any blood or anything," Helen consoled him.

"There's some chipped paint on the window ledge, but that could be from when I crawled through. I may have wiped footprints other than mine off the floor as well. Has Cuthbert returned yet?"

"No, but Estelle doesn't seem too concerned. She's taking a nap in her room. The Allerdice family minus Donnie is playing cards in the living room. I made them some cocoa and banked up the fire. Alistair is in the library watching the news."

"I shall take a walk around the property, see if I can't find Cuthbert and the boy. I'd like to have a word with each of them."

"Don't go far," Helen begged. "I don't know which of the guests murdered Moira."

"You're safe enough. Just don't go near Alistair."

Helen jumped at his words. "What do you mean, Rex? Surely—"

"Just stay in public view, lass, and you'll be fine."

SIXTEEN

REX HEADED OUT OF doors, planning to find somewhere out of earshot of the guests and away from prying eyes. While skirting the gorse-decked loch, he noticed what looked like a jellyfish. On closer inspection, he found it to be a plastic shower cap, such as Moira had been accustomed to wear in the bath. Grabbing a twig, he dragged it out of the cold gray water and wrapped it in a clean handkerchief.

Hoping against hope that her phone had enough charge left in the battery, he continued up the hill where he might get a good signal. Sheltered from the wind behind a stand of conifer, he called his legal contact in London whose services he had used before.

"Thaddeus, sorry to call you on the weekend," he said.

"Mr. Graves, sir, I'm delighted to hear from you. How are you?"

"Just fine, but I'm up at my Highland retreat without a laptop or charger for the mobile and I don't know how long it will hold out."

"Do you have a land line, sir?"

"It's been cut."

"Oh, I see. Well, you had better just tell me what you need and where I can reach you."

Rex gave him the details of the drowning at Loch Lochy two summers ago and the names of the people involved. He added those of his guests he knew less well. "See what you can come up with," he instructed the young law clerk. "And dig deep into these peoples' backgrounds."

A clerk for one of Rex's ex-colleagues at the prestigious London firm of Browne, Quiggley & Squire, Thaddeus was an excellent researcher with highly placed connections. He was also discreet and therefore a perfect ally in his private cases. Rex gave him the numbers for both Moira's and Shona's phones and stressed the urgency of the situation before terminating the call.

Consulting the card Alistair had given him, he punched in the numbers for the coroner in the hope she had already had a chance to examine Moira's body.

"Dr. Macleod speaking," answered an older woman's voice, brisk but kindly, with only a hint of Scottish.

"Rex Graves, QC. I'm calling aboot the victim pulled from the loch at Gleaneagle Lodge. My colleague Alistair Frazer supplied the information to the medics."

"Are you a relation of Moira Wilcox?"

"No, just a good friend. She was staying at my house." He gave Sheila Macleod the whereabouts of Moira's father in Glasgow so the police could inform him of her death. "I wonder if you might let me have a few details if you've had time to look at the body."

"I have, and I can tell you I've examined several drownings in lochs. In fact, I published a medical article on the subject last year. In a smaller, slightly brackish lake like Loch Lown, you might find some effects of hypertonicity in the victim's blood and lungs, indicative of salt concentration. Not so in this case, and no aspiration or ingestion of any vegetation or other particulate matter, although I found aquatic debris in the victim's hair. I would therefore be inclined to concur with the theory provided by Mr. Frazer that this drowning took place in the bathtub."

Adjusting the phone to his ear, Rex perched on a damp log, green and springy with clinging moss. "What else did you find, doctor?" he asked with all the reverence he could infuse in his voice.

"Hip fracture consistent with a heavy fall. The bloodless scratches on her hand also occurred postmortem. The blood clots quickly once the heart shuts down, as I'm sure you're aware."

"So following my assumption, she was dead before she was pushed out the window?"

"Before she sustained her injuries, yes. A bruise inflicted post mortem, as on Moira's hip, will contain the normal count of white blood cells and no more. This is because extra white blood cells only rush to the site of an injury to start the healing process while the body is still living."

"Any other forensic clues?"

"I was not able to lift any prints, I'm afraid. Nor much else. I would guess—and this won't go into my report because it is only a guess—that if the victim was murdered, someone pushed her head under the water. Not much force would have been required if she panicked and slipped."

"Right," Rex concurred. "There was a lot of water on the floor, but that could have been from sudden displacement of the water when she went under, rather than a struggle. I didn't see any marks around her throat or anything. No one heard anything either."

"I have just begun to catalogue the injuries," the doctor informed him. "But the ones I mentioned are the most obvious. The trauma to her right hip might just conceivably have been caused by striking a rock when she was released into the loch, but it's rather uniform, so I think a flat surface where she made contact is more likely. So far, I have noted an elevated level of alcohol in her system, which may have slowed her reactions when confronted by an alleged assailant. That's all I have for the time being."

"I'm most grateful to you, doctor."

After Rex ended the call, he thoughtfully tapped the phone against his chin. Dr. Macleod had not come up with any great surprises, but it was reassuring to have his theories substantiated by an expert. He could now proceed with more confidence.

Meeting Helen at the front door, where she was anxiously waiting, he asked, "Do you fancy a walk? I need to round up Cuthbert and Donnie."

"I thought that's where you went."

"I had other business to attend to first."

"I'll just get my anorak." She disappeared back inside and re-emerged dressed for the elements. "I was getting worried."

He pulled her away from the house. "I found Moira's mobile—"

"Where?" Helen demanded.

"Hidden in the coal shed. But don't let on."

At that moment a window squeaked open above them. "Are you going out to look for Bertie?" Estelle blared out from the guest bedroom.

"Aye. If he returns in our absence, tell him to stay put. Same goes for Donnie."

"I could come with you. I'll be ready in a jiffy."

"We won't be long," Rex answered, moving on his way. The window slammed behind him. "She doesn't sound pleased we're going without her."

"I couldn't bear it if she came along. She's so bossy! Why are we going this way?" Helen asked, hurrying after him.

"It's most likely Cuthbert went back to the spot where Donnie saw the hummel yesterday, over in Deer Glen."

A quarter of a mile uphill, they crossed a wooden footbridge spanning a burn and followed upstream as it pursued its ghostly trickle past lonely mountain ash and grassy fringes rampant with harebell.

"I'm still a bit stumped," Rex admitted, leading the way along the bank. "I think I've narrowed down who might have killed Moira. I just don't know for sure."

"Perhaps I could help."

"Who do *you* think murdered Moira?" he asked.

"Hamish Allerdice."

"Really? Why?"

"Because he's a lewd scumbag who can't keep his hands to himself!"

"The same could be said of Cuthbert Farquharson for pinching your bottom, but go on."

"Well, I think Hamish came on to Moira and things got a bit out of hand. He might have gone back to shut her up before she said anything to his wife."

"Plausible theory. Who else?"

"It's Hamish," Helen insisted, beginning to sound winded from the exertion of climbing. "I can't imagine Alistair killing anyone, and Cuthbert is inept."

"The actual murder didn't take a whole lot of brains."

Helen turned to face him. "Then why haven't you outed the suspect yet? All you'd have to do is tell the person you knew exactly how they did it and wring a confession out of them."

"The problem is," Rex said, taking this opportunity for a break and filling his pipe, "the murder could have been executed by any one of them, except for perhaps one thing—maybe two. And the question of motive."

"What two things?"

Rex tamped down the Clan tobacco with his thumb. "First, I need you to help me walk through this, in case I missed something."

"Unlikely—but okay..."

"I think we can eliminate Alistair from our list of suspects."

"But you said to keep away from him."

"Aye, and I still want you to do that. But he's the only guest who, to my knowledge, has been here before."

"Wouldn't that give him an advantage?"

Rex sucked on his pipe stem and blew out a ring of smoke. "The islet," he said at length.

"What about it?"

"The person who disposed of Moira's body can't have known about the islet when they dumped her in the middle of the loch. Too much risk of the body getting washed up, which is what happened. But with all the rain, the murderer wouldn't have seen it."

"I suppose," Helen conceded. "However, the Farquharsons came just before the rain started, so they might have seen the island, even though it is quite a way off. That's if they were paying attention. All Cuthbert could think about was going after deer. And Estelle was talking nineteen to the dozen and wouldn't have noticed if the monster of Loch Lown had done an impersonation of Free Willy right in front of her."

Rex chuckled at the vision of the killer whale, transformed into Bessie, vaulting the barricade to freedom. "Estelle is strong enough to have hoisted Moira's body through the bathroom window," he pointed out. "And Flora described someone fitting her description appearing on the stairs with a weapon. She could have used it to threaten Moira."

"I've got it!" Helen cried out in excitement. "Estelle knocked at the bathroom door, using some pretext to get Moira out of the bath and then forced her back into it and drowned her."

"Continue."

"Then she pushed Moira's body out the window and got herself down somehow ... Perhaps the ladder was already in place. All she had to do then was drag the body into the boat and row it out onto the lake."

"No drag marks," Rex pointed out. "A dead body would have made deep tracks in the lawn, which even the rain couldn't wash away."

"She used a twig or something to get rid of them."

"No time. Someone might have noticed her disappearance."

"Well, I don't really think it was her, anyway. I can't think of a reason for Estelle to kill Moira, except that her chump of a husband was playing the gallant knight to the poor damsel in distress.

And Flora and Shona don't have the gumption. So other than Hamish, we're left with that oddball Rob Roy, whose only interest is loch monsters, and Donnie. But he's as slow-witted as Cuthbert is inept. Plus he roams the glens. He might have known about the island in the loch."

"What aboot a complete stranger to these parts?"

"Who? Oh, you mean the man at the Gleneagle Arms wearing something on his head? The barman said he entered the pub at nine o'clock last night and asked for directions to the lodge."

"That was probably Moira's cab driver. She told me they got lost. That might explain why the man was in a bad mood. He'd driven all the way from Edinburgh. It was dark and raining, and he had no doubt been given the runaround by the xenophobic villagers. Still, the fact that he was wearing something unspecified on his head, perhaps to protect him from the rain, is curious…"

They resumed their walk. The path, cutting through Scots pine, branched off to the left and then rose steadily to give a bird's-eye view of Loch Lown, looking remote and secretive as it pointed its long pale finger of water. Beyond, on the northern slopes, sheep grazed in upland pastures dotted with scree and cairns of gray rock. Farther away, the moors rose in a brown and green camouflage pattern, while in the far distance soared misty-topped mountains clad in native Caledonian pine and stippled with waterfalls.

"Come on." Rex told Helen, turning his back to the loch and house. "There will be plenty of time for sightseeing later. I hope."

That's when they saw it. In a clearing on a hillside, no more than thirty yards away, a stag with fourteen points on its new antlers stood motionless and regal, its reddish-brown hair matted almost black from the rain.

"Isn't he beautiful?" Helen said in an awed breath.

"It's an Imperial. Don't move a muscle now."

Suddenly a shot rang out in the still silence. The stag reared and bolted into the forest.

"Is he hurt?" Helen cried, staring after it.

"I don't think so, but I'll hurt the person who fired. Sounds like the shot came from over there. Keep your head down."

Shielding Helen, he plunged into the bracken.

SEVENTEEN

THEY WALKED SEVERAL PACES, the wet branches cracking dully beneath their feet and seeming to echo among the tall pine trees, making it impossible to conceal their whereabouts. Fallen logs and tangled tussocks of undergrowth conspired to trip them up at every turn.

"Over here!" called a weak male voice. "I'm hurt."

Rex and Helen picked up speed and found Cuthbert in a clearing slumped against a gnarled tree stump.

"What happened?" Rex demanded.

Cuthbert raised his head. "I sprained my ankle when I fell into a blasted bog. I've been stuck here waiting for a search party. Where the devil have you been? I need to get this ankle on ice before it puffs up."

"Did you shoot at that stag?" Rex asked, quite willing to leave Cuthbert in his misery for a while longer.

"I did not. I heard voices in the forest and fired off a shot to alert you as to where I was. I haven't seen any bloody deer all day."

"Have you seen Donnie?"

"No, now get me up and out of here. Please."

Rex appraised Cuthbert's small, if dense size. The path back to the lodge led over diverse terrain and was too uneven for the three of them to walk abreast supporting Cuthbert between them.

"It won't be easy," Rex said, thinking about sending Helen back to the house for Hamish and bringing some sort of makeshift stretcher.

However, he didn't like the idea of Helen roaming about the hills by herself, nor did he much like the idea of leaving her here while he went back. All the same, he knew the way better and Cuthbert had the gun in case he and Helen were confronted by a wild boar or other threat. Rex had read in *The Times* that wild boar, extinct before the seventeenth century, were being reintroduced into the Highlands in a forestry regeneration project and, while he applauded this environmental effort, he still wouldn't want to come face to snout with one of these large, hairy beasts.

"Helen, I should go and get help from the house. I'll be as quick as I can. Will—"

He was interrupted by a loud crashing of disturbed branches and the stomp of feet approaching through the bracken. Pine twigs quivered, wet ferns parted, and Donnie stepped into the clearing with Honey in tow.

"Lad, am I pleased to see you," Rex said over the thumping of his heart. "We have a minor emergency. Cuthbert is lame and needs a ride back to the lodge."

"I heard the shot," Donnie said. "Did ye shoot yerself in the foot, Mr. Farquharson?"

"I did not!"

"He just sprained it," Rex informed him.

"Where were you, boy?" Cuthbert demanded. "I'll die of hypothermia if I sit out here any longer."

"Och, it's not that cold," Rex told him.

"It's damp. I can feel it in my bones."

"Well, let's get you onto the pony."

"There's no saddle," Cuthbert objected. "And no stirrups. How will I keep my balance? I can't risk falling on this bum ankle."

"What a baby," Helen murmured to Rex.

"If you'd stayed at the lodge, like I asked you, this would never have happened." Rex pulled him to his feet—or, more specifically, to his one good foot.

"Estelle was driving me bonkers. I had to get out of there. We have separate wings at our castle in Fife."

"We'll lay him across the pony," Donnie suggested. "Jist like a trussed deer."

"What, on my stomach?" Cuthbert protested.

"It's safest."

Rex trusted the lad's judgment in this matter. The position had the added advantage of making it hard for Cuthbert to speak. Mr. Farquharson hobbled over to the sturdy animal, which snorted and shook its head and neck with vigor. Donnie held the reins firmly and coaxed her with soft words in Gaelic.

"Over you go, Mr. Farquharson," he instructed. "Honey is plenty shaggy under the belly. Jist hold on tight."

Rex took Helen aside. "We're aboot halfway to the Loch Lochy Hotel. I shall press on." He had questions for Cuthbert regarding his conversation with Moira last night, but they would have to wait until he got back to the lodge.

"Can I come?" Helen pleaded.

"Not this time, lass. I can make it faster on my own. Don't tell the others where I'm going. Tell them I went to see if the stag fell in the woods."

"Why are you going to the hotel?"

"Less you know, the better. You may inadvertently give something away."

"We're ready, Mr. Graves," the lad called out.

Cuthbert, arranged like a stuffed saddlebag across the horse's back, moaned and groaned pitifully, complaining that he would never be able to get his boot off with all the swelling. Honey swished her long tail against the swarm of midges, lashing her human burden in the process.

Rex managed not to laugh, but had a hard time controlling a grin. He would have loved to take a picture on the cell phone to show Alistair. However, he did not wish to advertise the fact that he was in possession of a phone. He reminded Helen not to mention it.

"Rex, you didn't tell me what the other thing was," she whispered anxiously. "You know—when you said the murder could have been committed by any one of the guests, except for perhaps two things."

"If you look closely, you'll see it," he said enigmatically. "You best get going now. They're waiting for you."

"You're impossible," she said in quiet exasperation.

"See you in a short while," he called out, waving them off.

Donnie led the procession. Cuthbert's winded protestations grew progressively muted as Rex continued in the opposite direction, bound for the Loch Lochy Hotel. What exactly he expected to find there, he could not say, but that was where five of his guests resided, and the others, with the exception of Helen, had spent time there at one point or another.

He had all but exhausted the leads at the lodge. The hotel might hold the key.

EIGHTEEN

By the time Rex stumbled to within sight of the Loch Lochy Hotel, he was weary, dirty, and dying of thirst after his second and longest trek of the day through dense wood and steep corries.

The valley that harbored the hotel would have produced a pretty postcard had the sky been less cloudy and gray. The wide loch, situated ten miles southwest of Loch Ness along the Great Glen Way, stretched almost that same length again. It made his own loch look like a puddle.

At the northernmost end, the two-story, white-washed hotel squatted on a grassy shelf above the water's edge. The building looked in dire need of a new coat of paint, the black letters of the hotel peeling off the façade. A pair of weather-bleached antlers heralded the front entrance, approached by a gravel forecourt and reached by a shallow flight of steps.

Slipping unobserved through the front door, Rex cast an eye around the lobby carpeted in olive tartan, relieved to encounter no one, although a medley of voices sounded from somewhere down the corridor. A pungent aroma of leek and carrot assailed his nostrils, spiking his hunger and serving to remind him that he had missed tea.

With an agility that belied his bulk, he darted to reception where a sprinkling of keys dangled from pigeon holes aligned on the wall behind the desk. Grabbing hold of the thick guest register, he thumbed backward until he found the entries from June of two summers ago, whereupon he tore out the relevant pages. Fully intending to return them to Mr. and Mrs. Allerdice in due course, he stuffed them into his anorak.

One of the pigeonholes contained a letter addressed to Mr. R. R. Beardsley, which he also pocketed. Swiping the corresponding key off its hook, he crept up the plaid-covered stairs and made his way along a narrow corridor, decorated with Victorian hunting scenes in cheap frames and grizzled deer heads staring at him through marble eyes. He stopped at room number nine.

With a glance over his shoulder, he unlocked the door and stepped into a room papered with faded roses and crammed with mismatched furniture that had seen better days two decades ago. The window afforded a view over the shawl of brown sand and shingle beach by the loch. An assortment of small pleasure craft roped to a short jetty bobbed over the sullen waves. Rex closed the curtains that suggested the dingy pink hue of garments run through too many wash cycles with non-like colors, and turned on the central ceiling lamp.

Beneath the window, a wooden kneehole chest of drawers with a chair drawn up to it served as a desk for a battered laptop. A pile of dictionaries, encyclopedias, and nature books, along with a stack of personal mail, towered pell-mell beside it. Rex unfolded the first letter, forwarded to the hotel from a Glasgow address two weeks before and originating from an editor at the *Inverness News-Press*.

Dear Mr. Beardsley:

   Thank you for your recent submission for an article on the Loch Lochy Monster. Unfortunately, we are not currently accepting ideas for stories on that subject, but wish you success in placing your article elsewhere.

   Yours sincerely...

Similar rejections accounted for most of the mail. The letter in his pocket was no exception. Beardsley must have inundated the national and local papers with queries. He had no reason for presuming on the Allerdices' hospitality if he could not reasonably hope to sell the Lizzie story and generate some publicity for the hotel. The man was a fraud.

Crossing the fitted brown carpet marred by a spattering of dark stains, Rex extended his search to the wardrobe, which swung open with a disconcertingly loud *creak*. A collection of clothes drooped from their hangers, most of them creased and giving off a whiff of damp and mold. One garment wrapped in plastic immediately incited his interest.

Pulling it out, he discovered a crisp scout leader uniform beneath the protective sheathing. His heart beating faster, he examined the tan-colored uniform.

He dove into the mound of sweaters and scarves on the top shelf, his fingers encountering, right at the back, a hard slimy surface. As he extracted a child's red plastic case, contents shifted inside. He drew a deep breath and, using a handkerchief from his pocket, set the case on the quilted floral bedspread. The catch sprang open with a few jiggles of the top of a wire hanger. He raised the lid.

His responses and reactions froze, suspended in shock as he gazed into the red plastic case. With the aid of the hanger, he flipped through the photographs. One in particular caught his eye. Kirsty MacClure lay in a bed of ferns, a bewildered expression captured on her cherubic face as she stared into the camera lens.

On the reverse side of the photo, in black ink, was written the name Jackie. "Beth" appeared on the back of Melissa Bates' likeness. Why had Beardsley used different names? Surely he could not hope to fool someone who came across them by chance.

In a corner of the case, he found a lock of flaxen hair bound by a pink ribbon, the same shade of blond as Kirsty's. Other mementos—strands of dark, light brown, and auburn hair, and bright trinkets of jewelry such as a child might wear—were stowed beneath the photos. Retrieving Moira's phone from his pocket and stilling the tremor in his hands, Rex photographed each picture with grim precision.

He closed the case and hid it behind the pile of clothes on the top shelf, where Beardsley had presumably thought maid service would never look. He bent the hanger back into shape and smoothed down the bedspread. No need to dally. He already had more than he had bargained for and more than he ever would have wished to see.

With an ear to the door, he eased it open and locked it behind him. He approached the stairs leading to the top floor where Shona Allerdice had mentioned the family lived. A purple velvet cord displaying a "Private" sign blocked off the steps. Rex stepped over it.

The first room he came to clearly belonged to Flora. A photograph of her and Alistair stood on the dressing table, the mirror reflecting back at him his mud-besmirched clothing and unshaven face. He returned his attention back to the photo. As he was studying it, a light tap at the door spun him around, and an elderly maid in a white cap and apron entered, and shrieked. The same woman had made up his room when he stayed at the hotel.

Rex held out his hand in appeasement. "Don't worry. I'm no a burglar," he assured her.

"Mr. Graves? Ye gave me such a turn! I hardly recognized ye," she said in a homey Scottish burr. "Have ye come from Gleneagle Lodge in the rain?"

"Aye, I walked all the way."

"Are the family still wi' ye? We expected them back last night or this morning, after the worst of the weather had passed. Did Flora send ye to fetch some things?" The woman looked confused by his presence in the young woman's room.

Rex lowered his voice. "They're all at the lodge. We had an accident last night, and what with one thing and another—"

"An accident!"

"The Allerdices are fine but, now that you've found me out, perhaps you can help me."

"Best come away from the private quarters then, else they'll have my guts for garters—unless they sent ye up here fer something in particular?"

"I was just snooping."

"Are ye on a case, Mr. Graves?" the maid asked, curiosity burning in her bulging green eyes. "I keep up wi' all yer cases. Och, the one aboot that beautiful French actress on that exotic island—"

"The Sabine Durand case."

"Aye, and the Christmas mystery at—where was it noo?"

"I need to make an important call without further delay," Rex cut in. "I was hoping to find a phone up here where I could talk in private."

"Come downstairs before someone sees ye. I get off in twenty minutes. Can I give ye a lift back to Gleneagle Lodge? It's not far oot of my way."

"I wouldna say no, Mrs ... ?"

"Phyllis. Phyllis McIntyre."

She took him down the back stairs and into a large modernized kitchen, empty of staff and redolent of the vegetables he had noticed before, stewing in a large pot on the industrial-size stove in readiness for dinner. By that time, they would be pulverized beyond recognition of their original form, as experienced during one of his meals there. Trays of dirty tea plates were stacked on the counter next to the serving hatch.

"Ye look like ye could do with a cup o' tea," Phyllis said, drying red-roughened hands on her apron.

"Och, you're a godsend. Could I use the phone at reception? I don't know how long my mobile will hold oot."

"Aye, go ahead. Nobody'll bother ye. Most of the guests went oot after tea now that the rain has let up."

Rex made his way back to the lobby and deftly replaced Mr. Beardsley's key on its hook. He then dialed the number for Chief Inspector Dalgerry, who was heading up the Moor murders investigation. He had met the dour Scotsman on one occasion in the course of his work. Dalgerry was like a dog with a bone when it came to pursuing a lead, often loath to give up one favorite bone while other leads went ignored. It could prove difficult to persuade him that the traveling salesman in his custody might not be the child abductor after all.

Refusing to leave a message with a subordinate, Rex finally got through to Dalgerry's voicemail. "This is Rex Graves, QC," he informed the chief inspector. "I may have an important break in the Kirsty MacClure and Melissa Bates cases, and enough evidence to secure a search warrant for one Rob Roy Beardsley, that's *e-y*, from Glasgow, currently staying at the Loch Lochy Hotel." Rex left his local address, directions, and phone numbers at which to reach him.

The chief inspector might even argue that the photos Rex found had been posted by his detainee and downloaded from the Internet. Yet, DNA testing of the locks of hair would prove a physical link to the victims if Beardsley was the culprit. Rex had evidence too that put Beardsley in the vicinity of Melissa Bates' murder, but he was saving that information for his grand finale.

When he returned to the hotel kitchen, a cup of tea and two buttered scones, split in two and filled with lumpy strawberry jam, were awaiting on a Formica-topped table. He thanked Phyllis profusely as she cleared the trays on the counter and loaded the dishwasher.

"I was surprised to see a photo of a colleague of mine in Flora's room," he said between mouthfuls. "An advocate by the name of Alistair Frazer."

Phyllis glanced at him over her shoulder. "Handsome gentleman. Stayed here in early spring wi' his solicitor friend. Flora took a shine to him. I think that photo in her room was taken at a wine and cheese event at the hotel. Mrs. Allerdice likes to photograph the guests for the hotel book."

Rex gulped back the last of his tea as Phyllis put on her coat. "Where does she keep the book?" he inquired, getting up from the table.

"Now, now, Mr. Graves. Ye'll get me in trouble fer sure."

"I won't. In fact, if you help solve this important case, I'll make sure you get some of the credit."

"Oh, aye? I'd be famous then." Phyllis hastened to tell him that the book was kept in the office and unlocked the door for him.

After what seemed like an eternity, he finally put his hands on the photo he was looking for. When he came out of the room, Phyllis was anxiously waiting for him in the hall, hopping from one foot to the other in her black lace-up shoes.

"There ye are at last," she said, knotting a head scarf under her double chin. "I'll be off, then," she called into a room off the hall. Sports commentary punctuated by loud exhortations in a foreign language escaped through the partially open door.

"There's only the cook and the waiter in charge here until the Allerdices get back," Phyllis told Rex. "The waiter is from Portugal and doesn't speak verra good English. But he manages to communicate fine wi' the ladies, if ye ken what I mean. Portugal's playing today. That's what my old man will be watching."

"I'd be watching the soccer too, if I could," Rex said with regret.

"My Vic tapes all the games. I could get a video to you."

"That's verra kind, but it's not the same as watching it in real time, is it?"

"I don't see why," Phyllis replied, closing the main door to the hotel behind them. "I catch up on my soaps after work that way."

"How long have you been working here?" he asked as they crossed the parking lot, reaching her Morris Minor in time for a renewed onslaught of rain.

"Four years, ever since my husband went on disability."

"So you would recall the drowning incident here at Loch Lochy?"

"Aye, it were dreadful!" Phyllis turned on the ignition and started the wipers. "Poor Mrs. Allerdice were a wreck after that."

"And Flora?"

"Och, she moped around for months waiting for a letter from her young man in America. Right scared she is she might turn into an old maid—at twenty-one! When yer friend Mr. Frazer stayed at the hotel, she perked up a wee bit. He took an interest in her watercolours."

"Mr. Frazer is a kind and sensitive man."

"He is that." Hunched over the wheel, Phyllis drove with caution, looking left and right. "Can ye credit all this rain? And we were having such a lovely summer."

"What can you tell me about Mr. Beardsley, the journalist?"

"Keeps to hisself. Doesna like to be disturbed when he's working, so I only do his room when he's oot."

"Is he gone for long periods?"

"I dinna ken aboot that. I do ken he sometimes comes back wi' mud on his boots. The guests are supposed to remove their wet shoes when they come in, but most of them don't bother. Now, the Canadians always do because that's their custom back home.

'Course, Donnie always forgets. But that lad isna right in the heed. Mental age of a bairn."

The countryside passed them by in a showered succession of pine trees and sheep-populated meadows while Rex pumped Phyllis for information about her employers.

"You can drop me off here by the deer fence," he said five minutes later.

"But ye'll get soaked!"

"You wouldna be able to take me all the way anyway. This is a shortcut."

"Well, off ye go, afore they miss ye over at the lodge. I'll no say anything to the owners. Here, take my umbrella."

"No need." Rex pulled his hood over his head and, thanking her again, ducked out of the car.

As Phyllis drove off, Moira's cell phone rang in his pocket. Seeking cover under a spreading oak, he fished it out and, flipping it open, saw it was a London number. "Hello?" he answered, cupping his hand over his other ear to hear against the sound of leaves dripping rain all around him. A bedraggled hare shot off into the wet undergrowth by his feet, startling him.

"Thaddeus here," the caller announced. "I have some information I think you might find useful in relation to one of your guests."

"Would that be a Rob Roy Beardsley?" Rex preempted. He listened attentively to what the young law clerk had managed to dig up.

Unfortunately, there was nothing to link Beardsley to Moira's death more than the other guests at Gleneagle Lodge, so they all remained on the proverbial hook for now.

NINETEEN

Rex jogged through the sodden grass and down the other side of the glen. The old stone lodge in the valley breasted the rain against a smudged green backdrop of hill and forest. Loch Lown stretched before it, lurking with its secrets beneath a shroud of mist. Would he ever be able to view the loch again without seeing Moira's body floating face down at the surface?

As he darted across the lawn, he was relieved to count all eight guests through the living room window. Helen, staring toward the loch, gave a sudden movement when she saw him. He shot a finger to his lips. He did not want to announce his presence to the others just yet.

Before entering the house, he took a detour to the stable to ensure Honey was safely inside and not roaming about wreaking more damage to his new plantings. Nor did he relish the prospect of rounding her up. A more ill-natured creature he had yet to encounter outside captivity. She only seemed content when she was munching on something—preferably something of his.

Recovering his breath after the sprint across the glen, he peered through the small window at the near end of the stable and managed to glimpse the pony's honey-hued rump sticking out from the stall. About to turn away, a gaping white-washed space among the gardening equipment caught his eye. The scythe was missing.

Mr. Dean, the gardener from the village, did not come on weekends. Who then had taken it? Perhaps a logical and innocent explanation existed for the scythe's disappearance. Instinct, however, told Rex otherwise.

Pulling open one of the double doors to the stable, he penetrated the murky gloom, guided by the snorting of the pony. The electricity had never been connected to the out buildings. On an overcast afternoon such as today, scant light filtered within, and he proceeded with caution. He felt his way between piled bales of hay bundled with twine—in the nick of time avoiding collision with a long curved blade dully gleaming in midair.

With a gasp of fear, he inched backward to the doors and unbolted the other side, admitting enough daylight to lay his hands on an electric torch suspended from a nail on the wall. Beaming it on the scythe, he saw it was resting across a bale, the blade sticking out into empty space. He listened out for another human presence. Honey whinnied and stamped her hoofs in the stall.

He touched his forefinger to the blade. Sharp as a razor. Mr. Dean had sat on the old well in the courtyard just the other day honing it with a whetstone. The ringing scrape it made had almost driven Rex crazy.

A dangerous place to leave a scythe, he mused, right in somebody's path to the stalls. An unsuspecting person might run into it, or risk decapitation by someone lying in wait. He buried the sickle under the loose hay and went about flushing out the dark corners and recesses of the stable with the glare from the flashlight. A sudden movement under a heap of dustsheets resolved into a hump-backed rodent skittering into the shadows, trailing a long skinny tail. The horse snorted. Then silence.

Without further delay, he closed the stable doors before the grim reaper could discover that his deadly ambush had been foiled—and try something else. With a renewed sense of urgency, Rex crossed to the house, reviewing the identity of the intended victim: A limited number considering the location; who came to the stable? And how did this link to Moira's death?

Pulling off his boots and anorak in the hallway, he crept to the library and rummaged in one of the built-in cabinets where he kept his Ordnance Survey maps. The grids representing 1 km on the 1:25,000 Series made it easy to navigate in the remotest terrain. He found the location he was looking for along with the notes he had taken on his findings at the time, never realizing how important they would turn out to be.

The rare Dalradian limestone on Rannoch Moor, dating back 600 million years, yielded soil suited to northern felwort, bottle sedge, wild strawberry, and globe flower. Another plant, the Rannoch Rush was exclusive to the area, and he had culled a sample and preserved it in an envelope, even going so far as to mark the grid where he had found it. The plant was dried out now, but there was no mistaking the tri-clustered carpels and spiky, reddish flower. It was identical to the sample he had scraped off one of Beardsley's hiking boots that morning.

"Rex? Is that you?" Helen appeared in the doorway to the library. "Did you find out anything?" she asked in a hushed voice.

"Aye. The police should be here shortly. How are our guests be-having?"

"All right. Just a bit weary and bored."

"Well, what I'm aboot to tell them will perk things up a bit."

"What have you got there?"

"Some interesting bits of scenery."

"From your walk over to Loch Lochy?"

"No, from Rannoch Moor."

Helen wrinkled her brow. "I don't follow."

"You will," he assured her. "And stay within sight. I found some-thing grisly in the stable."

She gasped. "Honey? Is she ..."

"No, the pony is fine."

"Good. I had a vision out of *The Godfather*."

"I doubt it was a horse's head the killer was after."

"Moira's killer? Oh, Rex, you're scaring me." Helen melted into his arms.

He stood rocking her against him. "Nothing will happen to you, lass," he assured her.

He strolled into the living room where the guests slouched on armchairs and sofas. Alistair set aside his newspaper. Flora, curled up on the loveseat, her dun-colored hair spread over the gold che-nille cushions, slept soundlessly. Cuthbert Farquharson reclined in a chair with his sprained leg on a footstool, his hunting rifle propped up beside him. Estelle was in the process of wrapping a hot water bottle filled with crunching ice around his ankle.

Cuthbert waved a tumbler of liquor at Rex. "Hope you don't mind, old chap, but I helped myself to your whisky to drown the pain."

"I think I'll have a wee dram myself. Hair of the dog." Rex's early morning headache had not amounted to much, but it was still there, gently pinching between his eyes.

"You're soaked," Shona exclaimed. "Sit here by the fire," she fussed, patting a padded tapestry chair.

"Did you find the felled deer?" Hamish asked from a window seat, where he had been staring gloomily at the view over the narrow loch.

"I searched everywhere," Rex lied. "In case it was wounded and had limped off somewhere. No luck."

"My shot went nowhere near it," Farquharson rejoined airily. "I fired into the air when I heard voices."

"I had to be sure," Rex said, scribbling in his pad.

Stand by. Need to detain R.R.B. until police arrive.

He ripped out the page and folded it, then passed it to Alistair on his way to the drinks cabinet.

His colleague glanced up when he read the note and rose from the armchair. He hovered by the door under the pretext of refilling his tea cup. The others appeared too apathetic to take much notice. Estelle and Shona were stifling yawns over a pile of magazines sandwiched between them on the sofa by the fireplace. Beardsley and Donnie played backgammon on the floor at Flora's feet.

"We should have started back to the hotel when there was a lull in the rain," Hamish groused.

"In those shoes?" Rex indicated his leather loafers.

"Aye, well it's pointless staying here. No sign of the police or the tow truck. Services around here are a joke."

Rex poured out a measure of whisky from the cut-glass decanter. "Well, it's an exceptional set of circumstances. The police are busy with the murder of Melissa Bates and the rain has no doubt deterred the owner of the tow truck from venturing out."

"Isn't that what they're supposed to do?" Estelle riposted.

"Quite right, dear," Cuthbert advisably agreed with his wife's loud bleating.

"This afternoon," Rex told the group, "I continued on to the Loch Lochy Hotel, since I was already half way there when we found Cuthbert in the woods."

"How were the guests?" Shona asked, sitting upright on the sofa. "Is everything under control?"

Not for long, Rex thought. Once word was out about their journalist friend, pandemonium would reign at the Loch Lochy Hotel. "I did not see any of the guests, but everything seemed to be running smoothly. Your maid Phyllis kindly let me use the phone at reception. And I have your cell phone right here, Shona. You can call the hotel yourself."

"Did I leave it there? I was so sure I had brought it here. How silly of me."

Rex glanced around for reactions from the guests, but none were visible. Only Hamish responded.

"You really are soft in the head," he upbraided his wife.

"Did you try the tow truck company again?" Flora asked sleepily, raising her head from the sofa cushions.

"I did not," Rex replied. "I called the police about an imposter staying at the hotel."

Rob Roy's back stiffened at the mention of police, all interest or feigned interest in the game of backgammon abandoned. If Chief Inspector Dalgerry got to the lodge before Rex managed to extract a confession from Beardsley, the journalist might clam up as soon as he was recited the caution. He resembled the terrified hare Rex had seen in the woods. Or the rat in the stable. For Beardsley, however, there was nowhere to hide.

Rex checked to make sure Alistair was guarding the door.

TWENTY

Rex addressed Mr. and Mrs. Allerdice. "There was a guest at the hotel two summers ago who checked in under an assumed name, and who had not undergone his current transformation."

"How do you mean?" Hamish asked.

"It was at the time the wee girl drowned in your loch. She wanted to see the mystical sea dragon. I wonder who put that idea in her head..."

Shona snapped her attention to Beardsley and stared at him with a look of incredulity. "You? Amy was obsessed with the idea of a creature living in our loch," she began haltingly. "She would run to the window at breakfast and say, 'Good Morning, Lizzie Monster, shall ye come oot and play wi' me today?' You were staying there then?" she asked the hotel guest. He would not meet her gaze. "No, it's impossible. I would remember you."

"Aye," Rex answered for him. "Your guest Rob Roy Beardsley told me he had not visited Loch Lochy before. This turns out not to be true. Apparently, the lure of revisiting your hotel proved too great. He also lied aboot his writing assignment on Lizzie. The *Inverness News-Press* flatly rejected his query—weeks ago. I have the letter right here." He waved it in the air. "He couldn't get any publication in the land to print his story. He has no real writing credentials."

"Damn you to hell!" Beardsley cried.

"You first," Rex told him.

Hamish snatched the letter out of his hand and read it. "We've been had," he snarled at Beardsley. "You wee sponger—"

"Wait, Hamish, there's more," Rex told him. "Sit back down a moment."

Allerdice did so with a rude arm gesture at Beardsley and chucked the letter on the floor.

"He also lied aboot not having been to Rannoch Moor. But you have, haven't you, Beardsley? At least four times?"

This got everyone's unblinking attention. Rex sensed a collective suspension of breath. "You could get to Rannoch Moor in under an hour and a half by car from the hotel, taking the A9 toward Blair Atholl and Pitlochry, and turning off on the 847 or 8019."

"I don't have a car."

"A van, then." Rex read out the license plate number that the law clerk had unearthed along with Beardsley's various aliases. "Dark green. Verra handy for hiding out in the woods and generally blending in with the landscape."

"You'll find I have no vehicle parked at the Loch Lochy Hotel."

"Well, I know that. But I'm sure I'd find it near a train station around here."

Rob Roy did not move. "A green van proves nothing. I was at the hotel yesterday when Melissa Bates went missing."

"So you say. Shona packed a lunch for your alleged ten-mile hike to the far end of the loch. But you actually went to Rannoch Moor. That's why you were late getting back and coming here. You did not even have time to change out of your walking boots. I found a rare species of plant stuck to the soil on your boot. The Rannoch Rush grows exclusively on that moor. In fact, due to its rarity, its habitat is designated a Site of Special Scientific Interest. I would recognize it anywhere, unfortunately for you. I even marked on my map precisely where I had found it on one of my hikes, and it just so happens to be in the area where Melissa Bates was found dead."

"Could you be mistaken at all?" Shona asked, clutching at her wool collar.

Rex shook his head in apology. For once Hamish was silent. The others stared at Beardsley with their mouths agape.

"I could have picked that up off the mat at the hotel," Beardsley objected, looking about him for support. "The other guests go on hikes."

"I'd bet you also have incriminating souvenirs in your room back at the hotel. You seem pretty handy with a camera. I wonder ... Did you take pictures of Melissa Bates and Kirsty MacClure so you could take them out when you needed to relive your depraved fantasies? They were wee angels and you sullied them with your disgusting hands—"

Beardsley lunged for him. Rex struck out with his right fist and sent him sprawling across the floor, rendering him unconscious when his forehead hit the stone hearth.

"Well done, Rex," Helen exclaimed, eyes gleaming with pride. "Are you all right?"

The square contact with the side of Beardsley's jaw had made a satisfying *thwack*, though as far as Rex could tell, his fist was unharmed.

"Couldna've done better myself," Hamish approved. "I'd like to kick his head in."

"That goes for me too," Cuthbert said. "And I would, were it not for this blasted ankle."

Shona burst into tears. "It's all too much. I canna believe it!"

Flora flew to her mother's side. The ever practical Estelle Farquharson, who had tucked her feet in, away from the body, proffered a white cotton hankie.

Bending over Beardsley, Rex peeled off the fake beard and removed the spectacles that had half fallen off his face. Peering through them, Rex saw they had clear, non-prescription lenses. "No wonder he got so riled when Donnie snatched them last night," he said. "They were part of his disguise."

"He looks younger," Shona said, holding the handkerchief to her face. "I hardly recognize him."

"You weren't supposed to. This is how he looks when he's on the prowl for his wee victims." Posing as a cub scout leader.

"I thought the murderer would turn out to be a dirty old man."

"Children are often afraid of beards," Helen pointed out. "He does look much younger without it." She stared at him in disgust.

"You know, I think he may have had a goatee before," Hamish said.

"He did," Rex replied, showing him the hotel photo where Beardsley posed in the dining room with a group of young men and a tall waiter with slicked-back dark hair.

"That's Brad with Alfonso," Flora said bitterly when Rex passed her the photograph. "These three are students from St. Andrews University. I remember him now," she said, pointing to the man at the end. "He was by himself. Said he was hiking across the Great Glen. I wonder, was that just before the first wee lass, a redhead by the name of Lorna, disappeared?"

Rex remembered the raw pain of the auburn-haired mother as she appealed on national TV to the unknown abductor to release her daughter. The first of a series of distraught appeals . . .

"It must be a parent's worst nightmare to have a child fall into the hands of a sexual predator," Helen said in a voice trembling with emotion.

"The second victim was a bit older," Shona recalled. "Eight years old. She wasn't found for five weeks, by which time her body was so decomposed her own mother couldna identify her."

The wail of approaching police sirens interrupted further discussion. All eyes reverted to the unconscious body by the fireplace where blood oozed from Beardsley's forehead.

"About time," Helen said, wrapping her cardigan about her chest and moving toward the living room door. "I really can't bear being in the same room as that man. Thank God it's over," she murmured.

Rex thought otherwise. Everyone assumed the serial child killer must have murdered Moira, but what was the motive? Why attract attention to himself when he had tried so hard to escape detection? Rex bid the guests remain where they were and to make sure Beardsley did not escape.

"No chance of that," Alistair said, snatching up Cuthbert's rifle and pointing it at the prone form of the pedophile as though nothing would make him happier than to put an end to his despicable existence.

TWENTY-ONE

REX MET CHIEF INSPECTOR Dalgerry at the front door. Squat of stature and heavily jowled, he resembled a bulldog in a black rain cape. Behind him, blue and yellow squad cars with flashing roof lights swarmed the driveway as uniformed constables staked out the property beneath the drizzle. It looked as though Dalgerry had brought his whole task force.

"I got your message," he told Rex. "This is Inspector Strickler and Sergeant Dawes from Area Command HQ in Fort William." They flashed their warrant cards. "What do you have for us?"

"In here." Rex led the chief inspector into the living room.

Dalgerry's dark beady eyes roved over the guests and came to rest on Beardsley, who was beginning to regain consciousness.

"This the suspect?"

"Aye, minus his disguise. Rob Roy Beardsley, originally from Brora. Now lives in Glasgow. Previous conviction for child molestation in 2001. Sentenced to five years." Rex summarized the rest of the results of Thaddeus' research. "Abused as a child and put in a series of foster homes where he was rejected by the other children." Was this the reason for the name-switches on the photographs? Were the victims supposed to represent the girls who'd refused to accept him? "Cruelty to pets was usually the reason he was returned to the institution," Rex told Dalgerry.

"Where'd you get your information?"

"A reliable source in London."

"What evidence d'you have that this is the Moor Murderer?"

Rex showed him the photos he had taken of the contents of the red suitcase. "I stumbled upon these in his room at the Loch Lochy Hotel where he is currently staying," he said in a low voice.

"Stumbled?"

"I wasna absolutely sure of his guilt at that point. I set out to prove he was staying at the hotel under false pretences."

"I sent a squad car over there after I got your message."

"He said he had not been to Rannoch Moor," Rex went on to explain. "Other information he gave me did not ring true, either. It was hard to separate fact from fable. I had to go and see what I could find."

"You have proof he went to Rannoch Moor?" Dalgerry asked.

Rex nodded decisively. "He was at Loch Laidon. A wetland vascular plant, the Rannoch Rush or *Scheuchzeria Palustris* grows there. I found a sample of it on his hiking boot. I had marked on the grid map where I'd come across this unique specimen."

Chief Inspector Dalgerry examined the map Rex showed him. "It's within meters of where Melissa Bates' body was recovered last night." He signaled to an officer in the hall. "Arrest that man."

Leaping to his feet, Beardsley pushed the rifle out of his face and bounded toward the window, which Helen had inched open earlier to air out the room. Alistair pulled the trigger. A muffled click ensued, accompanied by the acrid smell of damp cordite. Two policemen fell upon Beardsley before he could smash through the glass. The guests were all on their feet, except Cuthbert, incapacitated by his sprained ankle.

"The gun must have got wet in the grass," he remarked. "Bloody useless thing. The dealer ripped me off! He assured me it was the latest in Finnish technology."

Rex took the rifle off Alistair. "Just as well it misfired. You're lucky you did not kill him." He glanced anxiously at the chief inspector.

"I wish I had!" Alistair lashed out at Beardsley.

Rex pulled at his colleague's arm. "Easy now. Let justice take its course."

"What if he gets off?"

"He won't," Dalgerry told Alistair. "Ample proof this time. A witness in the vicinity of Muiredge saw a man matching Beardsley's description."

"What was he wearing?" Rex inquired.

"A tan uniform, such as a scout leader might wear."

Rex nodded in triumph at Alistair. His colleague relaxed his shoulders. "At least I know now it's not Collins who murdered the wee girl. I don't know if I could have ever forgiven myself."

"Definitely not Collins," the chief inspector confirmed. "We grilled him for three hours. His alibi sticks. No possibility of him being anywhere near the scene yesterday. And we had to release our other suspect, a door-to-door salesman in his fifties who happened to be in the wrong place at the wrong time. This one looks verra much like our man based on the sighting and evidence so far."

"Beardsley has a green van like the one mentioned on the news," Rex added.

Alistair slumped with relief in a chair as Beardsley was marched out of the room in handcuffs. He flung his head back and closed his eyes tight. Then he flopped forward with his face in his hands and wept. Estelle declared him in need of a reviving brandy and got up to fetch one.

"Poor man's been under intolerable strain."

"I say, old girl," Cuthbert said plaintively, wincing as he adjusted his foot on the stool. "I could do with a refill myself."

"Did you bag your Rannoch Rush?" the chief inspector asked Rex, prodding him into the hallway.

"Aye, it's all yours."

Donning latex gloves, Dalgerry scraped the plant and soil samples from Beardsley's boot.

"This is his knapsack," Rex informed him. "I haven't looked in it yet."

Dalgerry pounced on the bag and, opening it up, sifted among the contents. He pulled out a hunting knife, a ball of twine, and a roll of masking tape. "Well, well, what do we have here," he rhetorically asked.

"He has a camera somewhere," Rex added.

"Any interest in joining the Force, Mr. Graves?" Dalgerry inquired, baring his sharp teeth in a grin.

"Och, I'd rather stay dry and let you lads do the dirty work."

Rex's chambers were eminently more comfortable than police headquarters, and most of his work did not entail trudging around in the rain. He filled the chief inspector in on Moira's suspicious drowning and told him about the precariously positioned scythe in the stable.

"Curious," Dalgerry responded. "More of Beardsley's doing, you think?"

"I canna be sure."

"Well, most obliged to you." Dalgerry shook his hand. "I'll be in touch. Strickler and Dawes will investigate the Wilcox case and take statements." He dipped his head at Helen and opened the front door.

Rex returned to the living room to see if Alistair had recovered, and was pleased to find him joking with the Farquharsons. Cuthbert raised his replenished tumbler to Rex.

"To think we were harboring a serial killer!" Estelle exclaimed. "Vascular plant, indeed! You certainly know your stuff, Rex."

"How's the foot?" Rex asked her husband.

"Oh, he'll survive," Estelle replied for him. "Alistair's medic friend is going to come by at the end of his shift to make sure it's not broken. As soon as that's done, we'll leave. This whole thing gives me the willies."

"I'll get that," Alistair said when the doorbell rang. "It might be John."

"Aye, it makes my skin crawl to think how that child molester was after Flora!" Mrs. Allerdice burst out, handkerchief trembling in her hand.

"I believe he feigned interest in your daughter to throw us off the scent," Rex explained.

"He tried to befriend all of us, didn't he, Donnie?" Flora said to her brother.

He nodded, staring at the unfinished game of backgammon. "Honey didna mind him."

"He fed her apples and sugar lumps, that's why."

"The tow truck is here," Alistair announced from the doorway. "Three men. The work should get done fast."

"Oh, good," Shona exclaimed. "I called the hotel on my mobile. The cook is in a stew." She hesitated. "I dinna want the Loch Lochy Hotel associated with a child murderer. Do you think there's any way to prevent news of this leaking to the press?"

"No chance," Estelle informed her. "The police will be there right now with crime scene tape and fingerprint experts. They'll be questioning your staff and all the guests. News will spread like wildfire. Soon everyone in Britain will have heard of the Loch Lochy Hotel. It'll be infamous."

"Och, noo!" Shona wailed.

"I warned you aboot him," Hamish told his wife. "I said something wasna right. But you never listen."

"Of course, you might get some business from the press. The legitimate press," Estelle added snidely. "There'll be camera crews filming the place from every angle and reporters waiting to interview you. You could be on TV!"

Shona looked ready to faint.

"We don't need any more adverse publicity," Hamish snapped.

"Oh, yes, I did hear mention of a drowning at your hotel." Estelle interrogated Mrs. Allerdice with a look. "Am I right in assuming she might have been another of Beardsley's victims?"

"Aye, I suppose," Hamish admitted. "If he was in disguise and had booked into our hotel under a false name, he cannot have been up to any good."

"I remember a guest talking to Amy about the mythical sea dragon," Flora related. "He said if she went into the loch, the creature would sweep her up on its back and take her on a roller coaster ride in the water. She might never have gone in by herself if Beardsley hadn't encouraged her. And I got the blame for her drowning!"

Donnie rose from the floor and sat beside his sister on the love-seat, wrapping his arm around her shoulder. "I could kill him!" the boy muttered.

Rex raised his hands in a plea for silence. "I need you all to be patient just a wee bit longer. We still have to address Moira's murder."

"Oh, I almost forgot about Moira in all the commotion," Estelle apologized, repositioning herself on the sofa. "Well, who on earth is responsible for that, then? Surely it must be Beardsley!"

TWENTY-TWO

Before addressing the remaining guests, Rex went to have a word with Inspector Strickler and Sergeant Dawes outside. As he was finishing up with them, Angus approached him in the courtyard and informed him that his crew had replaced all the tyres.

"Whit happened?" he asked, cleaning off his brawny hands on an oil-stained rag and then using it to dry his shaved head. "Looks like someone took a knife to the tyres. Is that what that police car is doing parked round the side of the hoose?"

Angus had missed the first arrest, and Rex wasn't about to get into it and provide instant gossip for the village.

"Why would anyone want to vandalize all these cars?"

"I imagine they didn't want anyone leaving the property."

Angus took in the enveloping hills and wooded glens, steeped in rain. "Aye, ye are verra isolated here."

"That was the whole idea when I bought Gleneagle Lodge."

"It's a wee bit different when ye canna leave, though. Well, I hope the rain holds off a while longer. The road is like a mudslide as it is."

"I'd offer you a dram o' whisky," Rex said in chummily accented Scottish, "but my guests drank it all."

"Thanks anyway. I'll get one at the pub."

"You didna happen to be at the Gleneagle Arms last night, did you?"

Angus grinned toothlessly. "On Friday night, every soul in the village is in there."

"Happen to remember a man coming in asking for directions?"

"A man wi' a turban?"

"Is that what it was?"

"Aye. Stopped his taxi right ootside the pub. A1 Cabs it said on the side, with the 131 Edinburgh area code. A woman sat in the back, all dressed up, fixing her face. I was aboot to ask if she was lost when the man dashed oot and hopped back in the cab again."

Rex thanked Angus for the information and asked him to tow the Reliant back to the village and return it to the fishmonger. After settling the bill, he walked back to the two policemen. "Find anything?" he asked.

"Just a load of hoof prints," Dawes replied. "And we found where the phone line was cut."

"Why don't you sit in while I reveal my theory aboot the murderer to the guests?"

"You're sure it was a murder?" Inspector Strickler asked, as though Rex might be getting carried away with the idea of murder following the first arrest. "We're investigating a death without having seen the body yet."

"Aye, I'm sure. I've already spoken to the coroner by phone. Dr. Macleod's autopsy supports my theory."

"Well, we'll be glad to hear it," the inspector said. "It's been a long night and a long day for the both of us, and any work you can save us would be a blessing." He clapped Rex on the shoulder. "Churchill is chuffed as heck that he collared the Moor murderer. Now he'll make superintendent for sure, thanks to you."

Churchill was Dalgerry's nickname, apparently. Rex didn't care if the chief inspector got all the credit. The important thing was to get Beardsley locked away for good. He led the two officers into the house and showed them into the living room.

"Any chance of a cup of tea for our law enforcement friends?" he asked Helen after the statements had been taken.

He joined her in the kitchen. "I'll have a cup too, lass."

"Do you think they'd like some of my ginger nut biscuits?"

"I know I would."

Helen reached for the cookie tin. "Are we going to find out for sure who killed Moira?" she asked, placing the milk jug and sugar bowl on a tray. "I hope it's Beardsley so we can be done with it. And, anyway, I don't want it to be anyone else."

"I canna guarantee it."

"Can you give me an itsy-bitsy clue? By the way, what was that other clue you mentioned when we were out in the wood?"

"The pony."

"So, the islet and the pony?"

"And, of course, motive," Rex added while they waited for the kettle to boil.

"Would that be money?"

"Moira didn't have any, remember."

Helen turned off the flame beneath the whistling kettle and filled the teapot. "What about someone wanting to shut her up, like I said before? That leads us back to Hamish, because Cuthbert is basically harmless when it comes to women. I mean, he'll try it on, but only because he thinks it's expected of an old country laird to have his wicked way with anyone who takes his fancy."

"You'll see." Rex grabbed a ginger nut cookie out of Helen's hand and bit into it.

"Oh, you can be so smug sometimes!" she fumed.

"You were a big help," he said, placating her with a kiss on the cheek.

Even so, a few details remained hazy and he would have liked to be better prepared. However, he could not detain his guests forever and the police officers were waiting. Draining his tea, he took up a position in the living room with his back to the window overlooking the loch. The guests fell silent and watched in rapt attention as he reviewed his notes.

"This morning we were involved in trying to determine who murdered Moira Wilcox," he began. "Then we got sidetracked by another case. To begin with the facts: the coroner has confirmed that Moira drowned in fresh water and was dead before she reached the loch."

He reiterated the events in detail for the benefit of the two officers seated in the room. "After Moira went up for her bath at around 11:45, I heard Hamish in conversation with her, a conversation which quickly turned sour as Moira tried to rebuff his advances."

Rex noticed a sharp intake of breath from Shona and rapidly moved on. "Cuthbert spoke to Moira immediately afterwards and may have been the last person to speak to her." Everyone's glance shot toward Cuthbert.

"Oh, baa!" Estelle expostulated. "Why would any of us wish to harm the poor woman?"

Ignoring the outburst, Rex continued to plot his course. "Alistair and I went downstairs and saw Shona standing by the front door, acting suspiciously. It turns out she had just been oot for a smoke. At 12:15, she checked her watch, concerned that her husband would find out what she was up to. That's when she heard the thud of a falling object. The timeline fits in with Beardsley's comment about hearing a similar noise soon after he went to sleep. Alistair did not hear it because he was on the landing upstairs at the time. The library, where he was spending the night, is just below the bathroom, so he would have heard it otherwise."

The policemen nodded, indicating they were with him so far.

"So, you see, there was a lot of activity in the house. Now," Rex said, pacing in front of the window, giving onto a misty vista of loch and isolated fir trees. "Between 11:45, when Moira went for her bath, and 12:15, when a heavy thud was heard, there was a half-hour period during which time the murder was committed. I did not hear how the conversation between Moira and Cuthbert ended, but she mentioned a draught, which in retrospect I take to be caused by the opening of the bathroom window, through which we may assume the killer got in. The sound may have been drowned out by the running bath. The window slid open with barely a creak when I opened it this morning."

"I say," Cuthbert exclaimed from his invalid chair. "I felt a blast of cold air myself. I thought at the time what a draughty old place this was and how glad I was that Estelle had packed my hot water bottle."

"The window may not have been open all the way at that point," Rex resumed. "Since there are no curtains or blinds on the window yet, anyone can look in if they got up on a ladder."

"This is giving me goose bumps," Estelle remarked, rubbing the arms of her sweater.

"How did your conversation with Moira end, Cuthbert?" Rex asked her husband.

"Very amiably," Mr. Farquharson replied. "She said she wished she had been my daughter because her own father was a worthless drunk and was never in a position to take care of her. Then she said goodnight as her bath was getting full, and she locked the door behind her. I went back to the bedroom and told Estelle all about the conversation."

"Your wife never mentioned anything about it to me when I interviewed everyone after lunch."

"Well, I knew Bertie didn't kill Moira," Mrs. Farquharson spluttered, "so I decided not to say anything. He was only gone five minutes."

"And your trip downstairs in the middle of the night—any positive recollection yet of having done that?"

The two officers leaned forward in their chairs.

"As I told you, I may have gone downstairs to use the cloakroom. I have been known to do that almost in my sleep."

Strickler and Dawes raised their eyebrows at one another.

Rex spun on Hamish, whose face flushed to a mottled ruby red. "After you spoke to Moira, you returned to your room. Your wife left you fixing the radiator and was gone five minutes for a smoke. That did not leave you enough time to fetch the ladder, get through the window, drown Moira, and dispose of her body in the loch. Unless you're a trained assassin." Mr. Allerdice's out-of-shape frame clearly did not fit the bill. "That's assuming your wife's statement holds up ... But let's accept her story about her clandestine smoke for now. And let's not forget Flora's apparition on the stairs."

"Look, old chap," Cuthbert interrupted. "I don't see you casting doubt on Alistair. I know he's a friend and colleague and all that, but he did seem quite pally with Moira last night."

"You're barking up the wrong tree," Alistair replied. "The truth is, I'm gay."

Shona sat bolt upright and glanced at her daughter, who had turned as pale as bleached bread.

"It's true," Rex confirmed. "Alistair had no interest in Moira beyond friendship. But I believe he was the catalyst for her murder."

Rex gave his guests time to digest this while he planned his next words. There was no easy way to expose this murderer.

TWENTY-THREE

"Alistair was the cause of Moira's death," Rex repeated for effect. "That's why I told you to stay away from him, Helen. The killer thought Moira was a rival for Alistair's affections. I did not want the same thing happening to you."

"A rival to whom?" Estelle asked.

"Flora."

"Flora?" Estelle stared at the girl, who sat still as a statue, eyes downcast.

"Donnie knew that she was in love with Alistair—"

"Me?" Perplexed, Alistair stared at Flora in turn, who flinched. "I had no idea."

"Moira was flirting with you to make me jealous," Rex explained. "Fool that I am, I did not understand what game she was playing until Helen pointed it out. Donnie did not see through her stratagem either. He thought Moira might take Alistair away from his sister. He knew Flora had feelings for him. He must have seen the photo of the pair of them in her bedroom."

Flora blushed to the shade of beetroot.

Alistair looked mystified. "What photo?"

"It was taken at a social event at the hotel in the spring," Rex explained. "I found it when I was at Loch Lochy this afternoon."

"I remember..." The veil of confusion lifted from Alistair's face. "A wine and cheese party. Dear God. I was there with Bill Menzies. How could Flora have possibly construed that I was taking anything more than a polite interest in her?"

Flora hid her face in her hands and began to cry.

"Flora had been disappointed in love before," Rex went on, hating to humiliate the girl, but seeing no other way around it. "Donnie saw her grief when Brad, the American visitor at the hotel, went back home and never contacted her again." He gave a final turn of the screw. "The Allerdice siblings are verra close. You said as much, Helen. 'Flora is a martyr to her brother.' And, in return, he would do anything for her..."

"Donnie!" Flora cried. "Oh, Donnie." She broke down and sobbed openly in her brother's arms.

Shona sat rigid, white as her daughter had been when Flora heard about Alistair's sexual preferences. Hamish covered his face with his large hands and rocked back and forth on his chair.

"Deny it, Donnie," Mrs. Allerdice wailed.

"I did kill her," her son responded in calm counterpoint. "I did it. I leaned through the window and surprised her in the bath. She asked, 'What are ye doing, Donnie? Were ye locked oot the hoose?' I told her I didna mean her no harm and to keep quiet. I was getting rained on so I climbed in. She tried to cover herself up wi' a face cloth. She was verra pale. I never kenned I had killed her until this morning."

Shona Allerdice gave a low moan. Flora pressed her wet cheek to her brother's.

"But Donnie," Rex said. "You knew what you were going to do when you found the ladder in the stable and opened the window. You hid Moira's and your mother's phones in the coal shed and cut the house line."

"I never."

"You took Moira's mobile from her bag in the hall on your way out to the stable last night. And you would have known where your mother kept hers."

"I never!" the boy insisted. "I jist wanted to take a peep at her in the bath. I was standing beneath the window and I saw her looking out at the loch."

Rex thought for a moment. "Then it must have been Beardsley who interfered with the phones when he discovered Alistair had been involved in the Kirsty MacClure case. I wonder, did Beardsley borrow your shoes, Hamish?" he asked. "That would explain why the coal dust was on your shoes and not his. They would have been easier to slip on than his lace-up boots."

Hamish shrugged. "I have no idea how I came to have coal dust on my shoes. Donnie wouldna've borrowed them. His feet are bigger than mine."

"It wasna me that took my ma's phone, or the deed woman's," the boy repeated.

Rex felt the boy was telling the truth. He did not see why Donnie should confess to the murder and then deny touching the phones. The fact that Donnie might be capable of planning the crime down to the last detail had, in fact, stumped him at first.

"What did you do after you climbed in through the window?" he asked the boy.

"There was a face in the mirror," the boy murmured. "It skeared me off."

"What face?"

"The devil's face, like a mask."

"All right, lad," Rex said, hoping to get him back on track. "You pushed Moira's head under the water, got her through the window, and carried her body on your pony to the loch."

Donnie said nothing. He just shook his head from side to side, eyes wide open. "She's deed, she's deed..."

"You're aboot the only person that can approach that horse," Rex told him. "That's what made me think you might be involved. It was the easiest way to transport Moira to the loch. Rob Roy managed to handle the horse as well, but he was the first person to mention the thud in the night, which I doubt he would've done had he been responsible for pushing her body oot the window. Also, he had no reason to kill her."

"But what about the intruder theory?" Estelle asked. "The bulky shadow on the stairs with a head like a Gorgon's?"

"I believe that was you in your bathrobe and curlers."

"Oh, you mean like those mirrors at fairs?" Cuthbert cut in. "I say, old girl—time to revamp the image, what?"

"Shut up, Bertie."

Rex addressed the guests. "Flora may have guessed her brother was involved, so she tried to cover his tracks by mentioning the shadow on the stairs. She embellished her story by saying she saw a weapon. First she said a knife. Then, realizing she might be implicating her brother who carries a sheath knife, she insisted it was a rifle. Everybody had access to Cuthbert Farquharson's gun."

Hamish's face caved in as he spoke. "I suspected what had happened when I saw Donnie staring at Moira's body in the stable and mumbling, 'I'm sorry' and checking her all over to see if she was really dead. Flora told me she saw Donnie on the landing last night. Frankly, I was aboot to tell you," he told Rex. "It's just that—well, my family has been through so much already."

"I know, and I'm right sorry, but Donnie will get the care he needs." Rex raised his eyes to the policemen as a signal that they could take the boy into custody. He had confessed voluntarily.

There was no more Rex could think of to say. He left the room and went through to the kitchen. Outside he lit his pipe. The sky showed vague patches of blue above the dark-capped hills, but the promise of good weather the next day failed to cheer him. He could not rid himself of the niggling sensation that he had missed something important.

Helen, slipping through the door behind him, wrapped a consoling arm around him. "I know how you feel about exposing Donnie, but maybe Flora can have a life of her own now. You did what you had to."

Rex sucked thoughtfully on his pipe and exhaled a swirl of smoke. "But for Moira's death, I would never have found out that Beardsley was the Moor Murderer. It was when I was examining the footwear in the hall for traces of soil and vine from the flower-bed under the window that I discovered the Rannoch Rush on his boot."

"You caught a child killer, Rex! The entire police force was out looking for him and *you* found him. Imagine the relief of every parent now that the face of the sexual predator has been un-masked. The—"

"Wait ... What did you just say?"

"I said, imagine the relief of parents now that the face of the killer has been unmasked ... What is it, Rex? You've gone pale. Are you ill?"

He put his hands to his temples in a penny-dropping moment of insight. "I think I have just made the biggest mistake of my life," he told her, rushing back into the house.

TWENTY-FOUR

REX TORE AFTER THE police car as it made its way up the hill. Waving his arms, he yelled at it to stop, though it was unlikely the driver could hear him from this distance. Flora turned her head and looked out the back window. Finally the car came to a halt. Rex ran to the front passenger side and motioned for the inspector to lower the window.

"What is it, Mr. Graves?" Strickler asked.

"I need to ask Donnie something. It's important."

The inspector pointedly glanced at his watch. "Go on."

Leaning into the car, Rex peered through the partition cage at the boy who was sitting handcuffed between his mother and sister.

"Donnie," he gasped, striving to regain his breath after his charge up the muddy hill. "Think carefully now before you answer. What did you do with the ladder after you climbed up to the window and spoke to Moira?"

"Nothing. I ran oot through the bathroom door, down to the kitchen, and then back to the stable."

"That's right. And your sister saw you."

"Aye. But she never told."

"No, she did not. She thought you might have murdered Moira. Tell me aboot the face in the mirror. Here," Rex said, taking the notebook from his pocket. "Draw it. I need you to free his hands," he told the officers. "Can you let him oot?"

"Mr. Graves, this is highly irregular," Strickler objected.

"I know, but believe me when I tell you Donnie Allerdice is innocent of the crime of murder."

With a gruff sigh, the senior officer got out of the vehicle and, bidding Flora get out too, helped Donnie onto the road and unlocked his handcuffs.

"Try to draw exactly what you saw," Rex encouraged the boy.

Donnie took the pencil and, leaning the notebook against the roof of the car, drew a triangular face and a series of lines depicting brows and eyes, a nose, and thin lips. He finished up with a fringe of hair at the top of the head and a goatee on the chin. The effect was indeed diabolical.

"It's no verra good," the boy apologized. "She drew it in the steam on the mirror."

"It's recognizable. It's Rob Roy Beardsley without the specs and full beard," Rex said, showing it to the inspector.

"Isna that the man who was arrested earlier?" Strickler asked. "I'm not sure I follow."

Rex turned to Flora. "When you saw Donnie—"

"He was coming out of the bathroom," the young woman said in a rush. "He paused for a split second when he saw me and then took off down the stairs. I saw the top of Moira's head in the bath and closed the door. I didn't know she was dead then. But she wasn't dead, was she? I really didn't know what was going on. I thought Donnie had walked in on her by accident."

"No, she wasna dead at that point. What about the shadow on the stairs?"

"That was later on. I was on my way to the stable to see Donnie and find out what he'd been up to. It was Mrs. Farquharson I saw. I made up the bit about the weapon when I found out what had happened to Moira. I wanted everybody to think a stranger had broken into the house."

By this time, Sergeant Dawes had joined his partner and was keeping a sharp eye on Donnie in case the boy decided to bolt. Shona had slipped out of the car and stood by her daughter, a hopeful look on her perplexed face.

"Gentlemen, this is not the person who killed Moira Wilcox," Rex repeated vehemently, gesturing toward Donnie.

The pair exchanged weary glances.

"Mr. Graves, it's been a verra long forty-eight hours." Strickler did indeed look done in, badly in need of a change of clothes and a shave.

"I know," Rex said, "but the crime could not have been committed by Donnie Allerdice."

"And how not?" the sergeant asked.

"Everything you said back at the house made sense to me," Strickler added.

"Except for one thing."

"And what might that be?"

"Donnie left through the bathroom door, not the window. Hamish mentioned that Flora had seen him *on the landing*. So the door would have been unlocked. When I went in this morning, Moira was gone and the door was locked. It was locked all night."

"Perhaps the boy came back for her and left through the window," Strickler suggested.

"No time. Shona Allerdice heard the body fall to the ground at 12:15 a.m. Just before midnight, I was downstairs with Helen, the Allerdice women, and Beardsley. Hamish Allerdice and the Farquharsons were upstairs when Moira went to take her bath. The window of opportunity for murder, probably less than ten minutes from when Cuthbert said he bid her goodnight, was too narrow for Donnie to make a second attempt. He must have just missed running into Alistair on the stairs, according to my timeline."

"So, who killed Ms. Wilcox?" the senior officer asked.

"I believe you have already taken him into custody. The reason Beardsley killed her was because she recognized him. He was convicted of child molestation seven years ago, when they were both living in Glasgow. Moira might have seen his face on the news. He was sent to prison for five years. The next time he molested a child, he made sure the victim would not live to testify against him. After the first three murders, he bided his time for a while and struck again only when Collins was acquitted in the Kirsty MacClure case."

"Could you not have figured this oot before?" Strickler inquired.

"When Moira said something about him seeming familiar, I thought she could easily have been mistaken as he's verra nondescript."

"Sexual predators often are," Dawes pointed out.

"Apart from the doubts I had over whether Donnie could have hidden the mobile phones and cut the line, he seemed the most likely suspect. He was absent much of the night, he could control the pony, and he had motive. I knew Flora was lying about the intruder. It's only when Helen talked about unmasking the killer that I understood the significance of the face Donnie saw in the mirror."

Rex referred to the illustration in his notebook. "The addition of a goatee suggests Moira finally remembered who Beardsley reminded her of. Perhaps talk of the Moor Murderer sparked her memory. We were discussing the Kirsty MacClure case last night. She must have drawn Beardsley's face in the steam to test out her theory."

"He was the devil," Donnie said. "He put a curse on her and she died. I thought I killed her, but I never touched her."

"I know that, lad. This is what I believe happened," Rex told the officers. "Beardsley slipped out of the living room by one of the windows. He knew there was a ladder in the stable because he had gone in there at the beginning of the evening to feed the pony some oats. But Donnie had beaten him to it. He followed Donnie up the ladder and listened in on the conversation. When Donnie rushed out of the bathroom on to the landing, Beardsley jumped in through the open window, forced Moira's head under the water before she could react, and locked the door before bundling her body through the window and following after her."

Rex nodded to himself as he finished piecing the puzzle together. "He guessed the boy would ultimately get the blame, so he helpfully pinpointed the time he threw the body out of the window, which was just minutes after Donnie had left. All he had to do after disposing of the corpse was creep back into the living room and pretend he'd been awoken by the sound. He thought he would never be found out because no one but Moira knew about his past, and there was nothing to link him to her murder. Donnie, on the other hand, had put the ladder beneath the window and had a reason to get Moira oot of the way. So Flora could be with Alistair."

"Would Beardsley not have noticed the face in the mirror and worried that Donnie had seen it and might say something?" Inspector Strickler asked. "Why not kill the boy as well?"

"He is a serial killer, after all," his partner added. "Or did the steam evaporate by the time he entered, so the face wasna visible?"

"I believe he did try to kill him," Rex informed them. "He must have been nervous the boy would say something. He set up that trap in the stable to guillotine him. But we'd need prints to prove it, and it's doubtful Beardsley would have left any."

"We'll put SOCO on it." Strickler looked Donnie over and sighed. "I'll take your word for it, Mr. Graves, since you seem to have all the answers. But you'll have to give a complete statement to the chief inspector. And the boy must stay at home under the supervision of his parents in the meantime."

Shona nodded and babbled words of thanks. Then she dragged Donnie back down to the lodge before the policemen could change their minds. With a shrug and a wave, Dawes and Strickler got back inside their vehicle and drove off.

"I was right worried," Flora said as she accompanied Rex down the road. "I thought Donnie had killed the poor woman so I could have Alistair all to myself."

"I should have thought it through more carefully," Rex apologized, "but I was up against the clock. I'm sorry to have put your family through all that."

"Is it true that Alistair is … you know … ?"

"Aye. I only just found oot myself. But there are plenty more fish in the sea." Rex smiled sadly as he remembered Moira telling him that very thing last night.

"Och, well, I suppose I'll be too busy over at the hotel dealing with all the publicity to have much time for romance."

"You might want to take advantage of the media coverage to try and exonerate yourself for wee Amy's death."

"How do you mean?"

"The reporters will be all over Loch Lochy, taking pictures of where Beardsley was staying at the time he abducted and murdered his fourth victim. Mrs. Farquharson was right. The newspeople will want to know every last detail regarding your notorious guest. You might as well explain how Beardsley stayed at the hotel two years ago, unknown to you, and enticed the lass into the loch."

Flora slowed down on the road, head bowed in thought. "You're right. But you know, I should have been paying closer attention to Amy. I'll have to live with that guilt for the rest of my life."

"Talking about your life, perhaps you should think about getting away and leading your own life, Flora."

"I was considering art college. Aye, I shall go away," she said dreamily. "But not so far that I can't visit Donnie regularly." She tucked her arm in his as they proceeded down the wet path. "Thanks, Mr. Graves."

TWENTY-FIVE

REX SHUT HIMSELF IN the library, preparing himself mentally for the phone call he knew he must make to his mother in Edinburgh. Outside in the hall, he heard the scrapes and thuds of suitcases being moved. He really should help Mrs. Farquharson with the luggage, he thought, since Cuthbert was not supposed to put any weight on his ankle, but Alistair and his new medic friend were there, and he really needed to get this conversation out of the way.

Mrs. Graves answered on the third ring in her refined Edinburgh accent. "How did the housewarming party go?" she inquired. "Did Helen use the lace doilies I made for her?"

"Aye," Rex lied. "I wish you could have been here, but under the circumstances, it's better you weren't."

"Och, it's a long way, and ye know I don't travel well…What do ye mean, it's better I wasna there?" she asked, suspicion creeping into her voice.

"Some rather disturbing news, I'm afraid. Moira Wilcox arrived unexpectedly and, well, she was murdered. Mother?" he said when she didn't answer. "Are you there?"

"What was she doing at Gleneagle Lodge?"

"She gatecrashed the party. I believe Miss Bird may have told her where to find me."

"Oh, dear. But, Reginald, how was she murdered?"

"Did you hear aboot the Moor Murders?"

His mother rarely watched the news or read a paper. She said she found it too depressing.

"Aye, we were discussing it at our bridge game this afternoon," she replied. "I told Elspeth and Winkie that the police force should put my son on the case so he could catch the evil killer and put him behind bars."

Rex cleared his throat. "It so happens I did catch the killer. He was staying at the Loch Lochy Hotel and accompanied the Allerdice family to the party."

His mother let out a small scream. "Ye had a child murderer in the house? Did he kill Moira?"

"It seems she recognized him from years back, and he drowned her in the bath."

"That's terrible. How is Helen taking all this?"

"She's bearing up well. She's a tough lass."

"I really like Helen. I hope all this murder ye get involved in will not put her off being wi' ye."

"I'll call you later when I have more time, Mother. What I needed to ask you was if you could arrange the service for Moira. Most of her friends are from the Charitable Ladies of Morningside. I'm not sure what will happen aboot the funeral. I suppose it depends on whether we can locate her father in Glasgow and when her body will be released."

Rex knew there was nothing his mother and her charitable lady friends enjoyed more than arranging a funeral. They would hold a flower committee, a readings committee, and a refreshments committee, and any other committee they could dream up.

After managing to extricate himself from the phone—his mother eager to hear all the details to relay to her friends—he went to attend to his guests. "My mother sends her regards," he told the Farquharsons. "And sympathizes with your ordeal."

"Nonsense," Estelle replied. "We had a ball. It really was very exciting, especially when you knocked Beardsley unconscious. I'm just sorry about Moira, naturally."

Alistair wrapped an arm around Rex's shoulders and gave him a squeeze. "You were fantastic. I can't thank you enough."

"I'm sorry I missed all the action," John, the young medic, said with a seductive smile at Alistair.

After depositing Cuthbert safely in the Land Rover and issuing instructions to Mrs. Farquharson regarding proper care for the ankle, John took Alistair off to the pub for a drink. The Allerdices climbed into their van and drove away up the hill, ready to face the media onslaught at the hotel, while a cheerful Donnie set off cross-country with Honey.

"I will never get on a horse," Rex said, waving them off. "They are the scariest of all God's creatures. I must suffer from acute hippophobia."

Helen laughed. "It's hard to imagine you on horseback," she agreed.

The sun peeped out between gray-tinged clouds, brightening up the landscape in a final effort before evening, and reviving Rex's spirits. "Alone at last," he said, watching the last of the vehicles disappear from sight. He breathed a deep sigh of relief.

"Not quite," Helen replied, looking up the road, where a battered gray van was cresting the hill toward them.

Shielding his eyes, Rex squinted at it. "Well, I'll be…It's the McCallum brothers come to fix the radiator."

"Wonders will never cease."

"Och, I'll never get a chance to give you this, it seems. Best open it now." He delved into his pocket and handed Helen a small blue velvet box, which he had purchased in Edinburgh and been planning to give her over the weekend at a propitious moment.

"What is it?" she asked, cornflower blue eyes flashing up at him in excitement.

"Open it and see."

"Oh! Rex, you didn't!" she said snapping open the box.

Inside, embedded in navy moiré silk, sparkled a diamond ring, its setting in the shape of a heart.

THE END

If you enjoyed reading *Murder on the Moor* read an excerpt from the next Rex Graves Mystery.

Murder Unveiled

———❦———

Mrs. Victoria Newcombe
requests the pleasure of the company of

Ms. Helen d'Arcy & Guest

at the marriage of her daughter
Miss Polly Anne
to
Mr. Timothy P. Thorpe

at
All Saints' Church in Aston-on-Trent

on
Saturday, 29th of May at 11AM

followed by a wedding reception at
Newcombe Court, Newcombe, Derbyshire

RSVP…

———❦———

ONE

"The Darling Buds of May"

NOT A VERY AUSPICIOUS day for a wedding, Rex thought as he looked out Helen's bedroom window, where a drizzly gray day feebly beckoned, and windy gusts rapped the branches of pussy willow against the panes of double glazing. Evidently, May in Derbyshire was no more predictable than May back home in Scotland, and Rex felt sorry for the bride and groom, who would be setting out on a new life together this very day.

Wrapped in his flannel dressing gown, Helen entered the room with a tray, which she placed between them on the bed before burrowing her feet under the covers. "You must have brought the cold weather down from Edinburgh," she said. "I had to put the central heating back on."

"It was fine weather up there when I left yesterday afternoon. Helen, you should have let me make breakfast."

"I felt like spoiling you. I tried to make your eggs the way you like them—soft-boiled, but not too runny. And the marmalade is homemade, courtesy of Roger Litton, the Home Ec teacher at my school."

She proceeded to pour tea into two blue china mugs. "I hope the rain will clear up for our hiking trip."

"Me too." A keen walker and nature-lover, Rex was looking forward to their excursion into the Peak District the following day.

"I do feel sorry for Polly and Timothy," his fiancée remarked. "But I think it's an indoor reception. Anyway, it may still turn out sunny."

"You are the eternal optimist, Helen." Rex took a more pragmatic view of British weather: Be prepared and always took a brolly. He cracked the shell of his egg with the back of his spoon, sprinkled on some salt and pepper, and dipped a buttered strip of toast into the thick warm yolk.

"Perfect," he complimented Helen on the consistency of the egg and, noticing she was not eating anything, asked, "Not hungry?"

"I have to fit into my suit," she explained.

"Och, it's not like you're the bride. All eyes will be on Polly."

"Including yours?"

"That's not what I meant."

"I know. You're just trying to be helpful." She deposited a conciliatory peck on his cheek. "I can't believe Polly is getting married," she went on dreamily. "And to Timmy, of all people. But he ended up doing all right for himself, considering he was such a sickly child and missed a lot of school."

"You said he was an accountant?"

"Yes, at quite a prestigious firm." Helen shook her head in disbelief. "Seems like just yesterday Polly was in my office crying and carrying on. That girl had so many problems."

"Were they childhood sweethearts?"

"Oh, no," Helen said, refilling their mugs. "Timmy was bullied mercilessly at school. Polly, on the other hand...well, let's just say she was very popular with the boys. While Timmy was being picked on in the playground, she was kissing all and sundry behind the bicycle shed. After she dropped out, we heard she was going with an undesirable character from Aston. So when we got the invitation to the wedding, we were all rather surprised at the school. And her mother is ecstatic."

"Have you met Mrs. Newcombe?"

"Yes, and she's perfectly dreadful."

Rex shot a look at Helen, his spoon suspended midway to his mouth. "That's the first time I've ever heard you speak an unkind word aboot anybody."

"I know, it's totally uncharitable of me, but you'll find out for yourself. They live in a Victorian folly—one of those whimsical places built by people with more money than sense. Anyway, the headmaster used to call Mrs. Newcombe in most weeks to discuss Polly's behaviour—her smoking on school grounds, the truancy, and so on, so I got to know her quite well. No dad in the picture, you see. He disappeared, quite mysteriously, while Polly was still very young."

"An only child?"

"Yes, and only an aunt in the family. I was so touched to get the invitation."

"It must be gratifying to know you had a positive influence on Polly's life." Rex checked his watch. "What time do we have to get going?"

"By ten-thirty."

An hour and twenty minutes later, they were getting ready to leave the house. Standing in front of the hallway mirror, Rex spruced up his ginger whiskers with a brush of the fingers. The silk tie Helen had surprised him with was the same cornflower blue as her tailored suit, and the exact shade of her eyes. He leaned toward the glass. Did the tie clash with his hair? No, of course not; Helen had perfect taste in all things.

"You look amazing," he told her reflection behind him.

Her blonde chignon revealed the swan earrings he had bought for her when they first met, that first Christmas at Swanmere Manor—the location of his first private murder case.

"You don't look too bad yourself." She adjusted the pink silk carnation in the buttonhole of his charcoal gray jacket.

The boutonnière had been sent with the invitation, a pink affair with scalloped edges and embossed in gold script, currently propped against the clock on the living room mantelpiece. Rex had an inkling a leitmotif of pink would run through the day's proceedings. He just hoped there would be a lavish banquet. He already felt peckish, in spite of the breakfast he had consumed. "How many people will be there?" he asked.

"Polly said it would be just a small reception for family and close friends, and a few teachers from the school, including Clive."

"As in Clive, your old boyfriend?" Hmm... Rex didn't quite know how he felt about Helen's ex-beau being at the wedding. Emotions tended to run high at such occasions, especially when everybody had too much to drink. Still, it might be interesting to finally meet the mathematics teacher and see if he really was as boring as Rex imagined him to be.

"Yes, Clive will be there," Helen said lightly, "as will the Littons. Roger was Polly's Home Ec teacher and sort of took her under his wing. Diana teaches history."

Rex speculated anew about the tie. Undoubtedly, Helen was keen to present him in the best possible light to her friends—and to Clive, whom she had flagrantly omitted to mention when she invited him to her protégée's nuptials two months ago.

He watched as she checked the locks on the windows and the bolt on the back door. "I didn't know you were so security conscious," he remarked.

"I'm not, usually, but there's been a spate of burglaries in the county. Not that I have a lot in the way of valuables, as you know. Mostly, it's big places in outlying areas that have been targeted."

Rex carried the gift for the bride and groom outside, a cut-glass fruit bowl that Helen had purchased. He couldn't understand why a young couple would require a gargantuan fruit bowl, and privately considered a toaster a more practical present for two people setting up house for the first time.

He held his black brolly over Helen's head as they started down the path to the driveway, at the same time attempting to keep droplets of rain off the white and silver wrapping. He opened the driver's door of her old blue Renault, which was marginally roomier than his Mini Cooper. Environmental concerns aside, he would not have opted for such a compact car had he anticipated frequent trips from Edinburgh to Derby. Next time he would take the train and save himself the leg-cramping 250-mile drive.

Installed in the passenger seat, gift perched on his knees, Rex pulled a map from the door pocket and located Aston-on-Trent on the outskirts of Derby, neighboring the canal village of Shardlow. Helen set the windshield wipers in motion and reversed into Barley Close, a cul-de-sac lined with 1930's semi-detached red brick homes, the sodden front lawns and early summer flowerbeds as forlorn as a date stood up in the rain.

Definitely not an auspicious day for a wedding.

ABOUT THE AUTHOR

Born in Bloomington, Indiana, and now residing permanently in Florida, C. S. Challinor was educated in Scotland and England, and holds a joint honors degree in Latin and French from the University of Kent, Canterbury, as well as a diploma in Russian from the Pushkin Institute in Moscow. She has traveled extensively and enjoys discovering new territory for her novels.